The Holiday Breakdown

By Leah Bonnema

This book is dedicated to Tineke Ouwinga, whose loving memory will always fill our hearts, and whose joyous rendition of *Silent Night* will always fill our ears on Christmas Eve.

I wrote the original version of *The Holiday Breakdown* during the first months of the pandemic when we were inside our apartment in Queens and desperately needed some cheerful comfort. I hope that it brings you some of the same delight and solace that it has brought to me.

Cover art by the incredible Chintya Purida.

This novel is a work of fiction. Names, characters, businesses, places, events, locales, and incidents are the products of the author's imagination or are used fictionally. Any resemblance to actual persons, living or dead, or actual events is purely coincidental.

Table of Contents

Chapter 1 - A Real Christmas Mess...1
Chapter 2 - There's Always a Scrooge 15
Chapter 3 - The Ubiquitous Christmas Coffee......................29
Chapter 4 - The Cross Country Sendoff...39
Chapter 5 - The Breakdown I...45
Chapter 6 - The Kindness of Strangers...53
Chapter 7 - Pancakes and Panic Attacks......................................71
Chapter 8 - He Got Puns...83
Chapter 9 - Christmas Fairs Do Make a Girl Feel Impulsive .93
Chapter 10 - Ho Ho Ho..121
Chapter 11 - The Cross Country Ski Center......................147
Chapter 12 - Trim that Tree..161
Chapter 13 - Actually, Just Like the Prime Minister............173
Chapter 14 - The Breakdown II 185
Chapter 15 - Finally, A Cookie Baking Montage!.................201
Chapter 16 - Who's Rosemary Clooney Now 209
Chapter 17 - A Change in Perspective...................................217
Chapter 18 - What is This? A Chick Flick?!.........................223
Chapter 19 - At Dawn from the East...239
Chapter 20 - A Disheveled Whimsey PST.........................251
Chapter 21 - Christmas Eve 257
Chapter 22 - The Protagonist in a Christmas Romance.........269

Chapter 1 - A Real Christmas Mess

*M*ae Robards stumbled in the door of her Los Angeles apartment. Her dog, Scarpetta, bound in behind her excited by the promise of breakfast. Mae dropped the leash, kicked off her shoes, and beelined to the kitchen where she was welcomed by the smell of the coffee she'd left to brew. Mae felt completely useless without her morning caffeine and was already on her second round of the day. The one time she'd woken up late and had rushed to take Scarpetta out without having that fundamental pre-walk cup, she'd ended up forgetting to change out of her pajamas. It wouldn't have been a big deal except for the fact that Mae slept in a shirt, and only in a shirt. The article of clothing in question had been a tie-dyed tee that she'd made at church camp in the seventh grade; it was swimming on a thirteen-year-old, but came in a little short on an adult woman! She hadn't processed what was happening until halfway down the block when she'd felt a cool breeze on her undercarriage. Mortified, Mae had rushed back to the safety of the apartment, telling herself that the neighbors she'd seen that morning probably just thought she'd been wearing a skin-toned bathing suit. Mae had not

1

made direct eye contact with any of those neighbors since. Nor had she ever left the house without coffee again.

After Mae filled Scarpetta's bowl, she poured herself another cup of percolated joy and glanced around the small Los Angeles home. It was the Sunday after Thanksgiving and she'd only just begun hanging all of her Christmas lights. Normally, Mae would've started decorating the day after Halloween (if Hallmark Christmas movies could kickoff on the first of November, then so could her holiday spirit). However, this year Mae had been so bogged down by writer's block that she was late to partake in the tradition that always brought her so much joy.

Mae's agent, Neal Michaels, had asked the publisher for an extension on the next installment of her detective series THREE TIMES. Three times! Never in her entire career, or in college, or even in grade school for that matter, had Mae been late on a deadline. Mae had a lot of iffy qualities, or so she thought. She was *slightly* messy, conceivably clumsy, and definitely felt like she embarrassed herself more than the average person. But being late, well, that was not like Mae at all. It was so unlike her, in fact, that she didn't quite know how to handle it. And, no matter what she tried, the words just wouldn't come.

As was her practice, Mae had left her phone at home while out on the morning walk, hoping the lack of distraction would give way to a flood of ideas for her book. Mae glanced at her cell and noticed a missed call from her mom. Sitting down at the table she put the phone on speaker. Her mother's voicemails were always such an epic experience that it felt as if Mae and Scarpetta were gathering around a radio to listen to an H.G. Wells broadcast from the late 1930s. Although she never knew where the broadcast would end up, Mae always knew exactly where they were going to begin:

"Mae. Honey. It's your mom… Gloria Robards."

"We know!" Mae chuckled to Scarpetta, who looked back at her in clear anticipation. Scarpetta's facial expressions exuded so much personality that Mae often wondered if she was a human in disguise or perhaps even an angel sent from Heaven. Who could say?!

"So, your dad and I…" There was a cupping noise, which Mae could only guess was her mom covering the phone, followed by a loud, "KURTTTTTTTTT, do you want to pick up the other line?!"

Mae shook her head and laughed. "He's gonna get the portable phone," Mae whispered to Scarpetta. After forty-five years of marriage her parents practically functioned as one unit. Gloria Robards was a vibrant and hard-headed woman who was forever telling people the endings of movies. Her father, Kurt Robards, was a very forthright and fair man who just couldn't sit still for anything, and that included talking on the phone.

"Hold on honey," her mother's voice continued. "Your dad is picking up the other line. He likes to get the moving one... so he can pace. Well, you know your father."

"The moving one," Mae repeated and took a sip of coffee. At this point it appeared that Scarpetta rolled her eyes but it was hard to tell for sure.

There was a clicking sound and suddenly Mae's dad's voice jumped out of the phone. "Hey Mae! Did your mom call ya?"

"Yes honey, I called Mae. I'm leaving a message for her now. Say hi." Mae's dad repeated the greeting. Scarpetta laid down on the floor and Mae could tell that the dog was giving up on this conversation already.

"Well, I guess we'll get right down to it..." Gloria Robards said. Getting right down to anything was quite uncharacteristic for Mae's mother who tended towards conversational backroads. "Your dad and I are thinking that we might want to sell the ski center."

"What?!" Mae yelled and leapt to her feet so forcefully that she knocked the table, disturbing both her coffee and Scarpetta.

The voice messaged continued as Mae's dad interrupted, "Well, maybe not *want to* but we are retiring age honey."

"A lot of our friends have retired..." added Gloria, clearly trying to convince herself as much as she was Mae. "And, well, it's so hard to keep up."

Mae yelled at the phone, "Why wouldn't you have told me this when we talked over the holiday?!"

As if they knew what their daughter's thoughts would be her mom piped, "We didn't want to tell you while you were at Thanksgiving with your friends. Your father and I discussed it..."

"Many, many times," added her dad.

"And well, we just can't do it all by ourselves, Mae. And we can't hire any full-time employees right now. Brian's been doing trails part-time for so long now, and... we'd need more help than that." There was a long pause. Everyone was very clearly broken up about the decision. Mae stared at the phone, speechless. Her mother's voice came back, "Mae, we don't know what to do but this seems like the smartest move. January, we're putting it up for sale." Mae slumped back down into her chair, shocked.

"We're very sorry to leave this on your answering machine, Mae." Her dad's voice broke through the growing haze in her mind.

"It's not an answering machine Kurt, it's a voicemail," corrected Mae's mom.

"Same premise, Gloria," rebuffed her dad, who was very familiar with his wife's penchant for specifics.

"Call us back when you get this," her mom continued undaunted. There was a pause and then, "We watched that movie last night, the one you thought would be good but hadn't had a chance to see yet. It had that guy, the one from the movie with the capes. SO SAD, he falls in love with a girl who ends up being his long-lost sister and…"

Mae threw her hands up in exasperation. She was about to start yelling at the phone again when Kurt Robards' voice piped back in, "OK! Call us back. Bye honey!" The message cut off and Mae stared at the

6

phone as she tried to make sense of the message her parents had left.

Mae couldn't believe they were going to sell the cross country ski center! It had been their entire life since before Mae was born. The family home was located on the same wooded lot in New Hampshire as the trails and Welcome Center. It was unimaginable to Mae that her parents really wanted to let it go. She sat there in contemplation of the unexpected and unsettling news until her thoughts were suddenly disrupted by the ringing of the phone. Without hesitation (or even checking to see who it was), Mae clicked on the call.

"Mom? Dad?"

"Mae! No, it's me." Mae looked down to see that she had just accepted a FaceTime from her agent, Neal.

Mae had known Neal since she'd moved to Los Angeles from the East Coast over a decade ago. They had a great working relationship—Mae would even consider Neal to be one of her friends. But, in Mae's mind, hardly anyone was a close enough friend for an early surprise FaceTime call. She grimaced at the thought of what she must look like and peeked at herself in the screen in an attempt to subtly wipe away any unwanted morning face boogies. Who was she kidding?!

Mae knew that nothing she did was ever subtle, so she gave in and committed to using the phone as a mirror for a brief moment. "Oh, sorry Neal! My parents had gotten cut off and… never mind. How was your Thanksgiving?" Mae asked as she tried to pull her mind away from the previous call.

"It was great," replied Neal. "We took the kids up to my mother-in-law's. Watched the parade on TV, overate, got into a fight about puzzles. You know, Thanksgiving."

"Yeah," responded Mae, refilling her coffee and sitting back down to give Neal her full attention.

"I apologize for calling you on a Sunday. I just wanted to start the week out with a bang," cheery Neal said. There was a pause as Mae checked her image again on the screen; she was pretty sure she had coffee on her nose. "So, I know you know, but I wanted to touch base now that Thanksgiving has passed. The publisher let us extend the deadline ONE MORE TIME but they aren't going to let us extend it again so…" Neal didn't finish the sentence because he knew Mae was aware of the current situation.

"So!" Mae picked up where he left off. "I better get my butt in gear. Neal, I'm really sorta almost done. I just can't quite figure how it's supposed to work out anymore."

"Well, Mae, it's supposed to work out that we have the draft in on time. You can always rewrite the parts you don't like. Just give me something, alright?! This will be your third extension. You've never done this before." A few beats passed as Neal's words hung in the heavy silence between them. They both knew Mae was struggling with something totally new to her. Something that was much bigger than just writer's block. "And one more thing," Neal added. "Peterson's Publishing is bringing in a new editor to oversee all the crime authors. She'd like to talk with you this week. I'll set up a meeting."

Mae straightened up so quickly that Scarpetta jumped to her feet again, sensing an anxiety storm brewing. "Okay. Um, about what, do you think?" Mae asked nervously. "That I'm behind schedule or…?" She let the sentence trail off as she momentarily got lost in all the horrible possible options of what the meeting could be about. That was one of Mae's stronger skill sets, give her an update and she could think of at least one hundred things that could go wrong. It really was a true art form of which Mae believed she'd be considered an O'Keeffe,

9

the best of the best, and a pioneer of American modernity. Only where O'Keeffe's medium had been paint, Mae's medium was overthinking.

"I think it's probably just a get to know you type thing," said Neal, knowing Mae's ability to jump to worst case conclusions. "We'll feel it out." Just then Mae heard a joyous yell come from somewhere in the background and saw the smiling face of one of Neal's girls as she bolted behind him. "OK, looks like I gotta go!" Neal said, all of a sudden very rushed. "Seems Alyssa is trying to put reindeer antlers on the cat. Happy official beginning of the holiday season to you Mae. Now get to writing! It's due December 23rd, and there's absolutely no flexibility on that! Oh, and I'll update you on the details of the meeting." Mae waved and the call cut off.

Hours later, as the sun was going down, Mae was still sitting at her kitchen table. She stared out the window at a silhouetted palm tree in the falling night sky. It was one of Mae's favorite things about living there. She was such a New England girl that she'd never quite gotten over the magic of the lone palm tree up against the horizon, especially at dusk. It always looked like a postcard to her.

As Mae gazed out into the world, she went over the day's drastic turn of events. She had pondered the current circumstances of her life that morning for hours and hours until, almost inexplicably, she'd called her parents back to inform them that she would be coming home to help run the cross country ski center. It was impulsive, and seemed illogical in so many ways, but in the deepest parts of Mae's heart, it felt right. Her parents, although worried that Mae might be turning her life upside down just for them, were happy with the surprising news. She told them that she could write from anywhere, hoping that the outward confidence would snowball into it actually being true. Mae gazed down at Scarpetta—their whole life was about to change.

As Mae looked around her apartment, she reflected on what a good home it had been to her, and how so many of Mae's adult advances in life had taken place there. The apartment was where Mae had her first very own parking spot. It was where she'd gotten her first washer and dryer. The apartment had come with hookups but it wasn't until Mae's first book took off that she was able to purchase the units. Mae had been so excited that she'd called up her best friend, Julie Chu, and asked her to come over and take pictures of Mae

11

joyously throwing dryer sheets into the air over the glorious appliances. She had titled the photos, *Making It Rain,* and had emailed them out to her close friends and family. The apartment was where Mae had been when she'd received the call that she'd won her first award for writing. She'd been so shocked upon hearing the news that she'd just stared, totally speechless, out the very same window that she was looking through now. Hours had passed before she'd finally called Julie and her parents to share the news that her book, *Finding Laela,* had won *Best New Detective* that year. It was where she had celebrated her dreams coming true. Mae glanced around at the framed accolades she'd hung on the wall for her (now) four book series. She was grateful that it had been such a good period of her life.

Mae was also so thankful for her dog, Scarpetta, who she'd met at an adoption day in the neighborhood park years prior. Mae had immediately taken to the pooch the moment she'd seen her sitting there with those big wide eyes full of excitement and hope for a forever home. As far as anyone could guess, Scarpetta was a mix between some kind of Australian Sheepdog and most likely a Dachshund. She had one blue eye and one brown eye, a sheepdog body, and little short legs that seemed to work at triple speeds. Mae honestly couldn't have imagined this time without Scarpetta; they'd kept each other company through so many ups and down.

Mae had had a smattering of relationships here and there while living in Los Angeles but, truth be told, it had been a while. She had yet to find a man who blended well with her erratic writing schedule, which was of the utmost importance to her. If Mae was honest with herself, she had to admit that she liked to be left alone whenever she wanted to be left alone, and it took a very particular kind of person to be comfortable with that. She briefly wondered if she'd ever meet someone who was right for her. She knew that for now it was just going to be her and Scarpetta, and that was actually totally fine by Mae. The two were both staring off at a beautiful palm tree and into an unsure future when her phone vibrated with an incoming text from Neal:

This Tues, Dec 1, 3pm meeting THE Elizabeth Birk at Peterson's Publishing. Confirmed?

Mae, who still chose to write things down on a physical paper calendar like some sort of time traveler from another century, got up to rummage through her bag for her day planner. She checked the date for Tuesday and texted Neal back:

Confirmed for Tues. See you there. Thanks!

Mae sighed again for what must have been the eight thousandth time that day. "Well, I'm not feeling too good about that!" she said to Scarpetta. Mae felt like she currently had more on her plate than she could ever remember having had at any one point in the past: she had to pack, to ship, to update addresses, to get rid of stuff, to meet a new editor, to inform her friends of quite possibly one of the biggest decisions of entire her life, AND she had to finish a book!

Mae strode over to her TV console where she perused an equal mix of fantasy and mystery DVDs. Yes, DVDs. She looked through all her favorite stories, the epic adventures that would pull Mae out of her mind and into someone else's. How she loved the power of a good story! Selecting her go-to calming movie, she grabbed *Lord of the Rings: Two Towers,* and looked over at Scarpetta for her opinion. "Only two people can sooth my soul at times such as these. You want Gandalf?" she asked as she held up the DVD. "Or would you rather Kurt Russell as Santa Claus on Netflix?" Scarpetta looked back seemingly unsure. It was a difficult call. "I know," agreed Mae. "Very hard choice."

Chapter 2 - There's Always a Scrooge

*M*ae and Neal were seated on a plush looking, yet somehow oddly hard feeling, leather couch in the waiting area of Peterson's Publishing's LA office. It was early in the afternoon, just two days after Mae's momentous decision. She had been busy packing, writing, panicking, and then back to packing again. Mae considered herself to be a great multitasker and found that with minimal effort she had even managed to panic while packing—a great two for one! What she had not yet done was to tell the people in her life about the swiftly upcoming move. Mae started to sweat every time she thought about it.

Mae looked around the reception area. There was no holiday cheer to speak of, except for a very stark looking wreath that hung over the entry desk. Mae eyed it suspiciously. "Seems minimal," she judged.

"Well, your standards for holiday spirit are incredibly high, Mae," Neal laughed.

"I gotta tell you Neal, I don't feel good about this." Mae said as she started fiddling with her pants. "A new head editor out of nowhere? An impromptu meeting when I'm late on delivery? Seems bad."

"It's fine. You're almost done the book," Neal said as he gave Mae a look which suggested that she indeed better be almost done. "Plus, it's your whole focus from now until Christmas, so you'll get it finished no matter what."

"Ummmmmm... about that," Mae began. Now was the time to rip the Band-Aid off.

"Uh-oh," responded Neal, clearly noting the change in tone.

"Yeahhhhhh, so long story short..." said Mae, still stalling for the right words.

"Now I'm really nervous," replied Neal in a joking manner that didn't quite mask the fact that he wasn't actually joking at all.

"NEAL... I'm moving home to New Hampshire." Mae pushed the words out of her mouth.

"WHAT?!" Neal realized he'd responded too loudly for the office setting and immediately lowered his voice. "Now?!"

Mae made a YIKES face (another one of her specialties). "Like at the end of next week," she admitted.

"You have a book to finish!" Neal threw his hands out as if actually trying to grasp what was happening here.

"I know," Mae said in what she hoped was one of her most calming voices. "I am *really* close, Neal. Well, sort of." Maybe not so calming.

"WHAT?!" Neal was now repeating himself. He was at a loss. "You're gonna pack up your entire life at the same time that you have to finish a book?! It's already December first Mae!"

"I know! I know!" Mae was aware of what a seemingly absolutely unreasonable decision it was, but she was standing by it. At least most of the time. There were those in between moments where she felt completely paralyzed by fear about the choice she was making, but she definitely was not going to tell Neal about that! "It's just… my parents can't keep the cross country ski center open without more hands. And, it means too much to them, and to me, to just… let it go? When I know that I could help!" Mae took a beat. "Plus, I think it's the right move for me mentally Neal. We both know I've been stuck. Really stuck. I haven't been myself for a while… and maybe this is the change I need to shake me back into it, you know?"

"Do they even have internet there?" Neal lightened his tone, slightly.

"Of course," responded Mae. "There's an IBM desktop all set up and waiting. They even flipped the outhouse in the backyard into a home office just for me. There's also functioning electricity, a flush toilet, AND spotty dial-up." Neal's eyeballs almost popped on the phrase *dial-up* but Mae laughed.

"OK," said Neal, clearly resigned that this was happening and that they would just have to make it work. "But, let me tell the publishers. I'll finesse it."

"Neal, you know how I feel about *finessing,*" Mae said as she made air quotes around the word, trying to drive home how she felt about finesses in general.

"I do," said Neal. "You're horrible at it. Which is why I'll…" Neal was interrupted as Steven Montero, who seemed to work not only as the office receptionist, but as an executive assistant to some of the department editors, stood up and walked over to them. Steven had been at the front the last couple of times Mae had come by and she really liked him. He was always extremely put together, probably the friendliest person in the entire office, and Mae sensed that he was ready to climb through the ranks.

"Elizabeth Birk is ready to see you now," Steven said with a welcoming smile. "I will take you both back." Mae and Neal stood, ready to follow him down the corridor to the offices.

As Mae walked down the hall, she tried to gather herself with a quick swipe of ChapStick, a glance down at her shirt to make sure she hadn't spilled anything, and a double check of her fly. After years of meetings where Mae had discovered about halfway through the conversation that something was glaringly wrong with her appearance, she had started pre-check list. Mae hoped that people found her seemingly constant state of chaos to be an endearing quality, although she highly doubted it. Steven pushed open the last door on the right and Mae stole a quick look over at Neal who appeared to be, as always, calm and professional. Together they stepped into the office.

It was a very modern and clean space with everything perfectly placed. There was a huge bookshelf up against one wall that was neatly filled with books. Mae noted that it was only canonized literature gracing the shelves and that the classics were, of course, all alphabetized. The office had one painting of a mountain scene and a framed poster of the Jim Rohn quote: *Don't Wish It*

Were Easier, Wish You Were Better. At that moment Mae decided that the meeting was definitely not going to go well.

"I have Mae Robards and Neal Michaels for you." Steven's voice broke through Mae's mounting anxiety.

"Of course, of course!" said the person who Mae presumed was Elizabeth Birk. She matched her office perfectly, in line and in order, and Mae gathered that the editor's business attire was not just an outfit but a personality trait. The woman stood up and walked around the desk towards her guests. "Mae! Neal! So lovely to meet you both in person. I'm Elizabeth Birk." She gestured to the two chairs in front of her. Mae eyeballed the *Wish You Were Better* poster one more time before sitting down.

"Would anyone like water or coffee?" asked Steven.

"Oh, no thank you," replied Mae, though grateful for the courtesy. "I'm so clumsy, I'd hate to spill it on anything in here by mistake!" Mae tried to laugh but the editor just blank faced the comment.

Neal pleasantly acknowledged Mae being Mae with a laugh and a smile. "I'm good thanks," he nodded to Steven.

"I think we're okay Steven. Hold my calls, please." Elizabeth Birk said signaling that it was time to get the meeting started. Mae immediately had to pee.

As Steven exited and closed the door behind him, Mae took a quick glance at the one personal item on Elizabeth Birk's desk. It was a framed photo of her and a very young woman at what looked to be a high school graduation. Mae could only assume it was the editor's daughter as the girl's face shared many similar qualities. But, while Elizabeth Birk was clearly a very crisp and 'coloring inside the lines' type, this other person seemed much more unconventional. A glaring difference that even Mae could discern just from a photo. Mae's pondering about the relationship was interrupted as Elizabeth cut through her line of vision and situated herself on the corner of the desk. It was intended to look like a casual lean but in that position, she was hovering over Mae and Neal.

"Mae, Neal, wonderful to have you in," Elizabeth began. "Peterson's has hired me to oversee all the detective and crime series authors here. I like to consider myself to be *The Peterson's PI Publisher.*" She laughed at her own alliteration. Mae started to not feel so well. "I want to be a little more hands on than the other editors here, whom I understand, have let you do your own thing for the most part." Mae didn't know what that meant exactly, so she did a smile mixed with a little light laugh combo in response.

"Well, it's great to meet you in person!" said Neal, determined to keep this conversation on a positive track.

"I've, of course, read all your books," Elizabeth would not be deterred from her opening statement. "I do love that Laela. She's so, what's the word everyone uses, quirky. So quirky, and dare I say, so emotionally disheveled. Very irregular indeed, for an investigator."

Mae's panic took off like a shot. She could feel her off-brand *YouAreSoFit* watch going into calorie counting mode, assuming that she was exercising because her heart rate was rising so fast. She glanced down at the watch to see that it was currently giving her a thumbs up. She inwardly grimaced and tried to calm down even though she knew the editor was not using words like *irregular* and *emotionally disheveled* as a compliment.

"We really appreciate the extension. Mae is almost finished." Neal's voice cut in before Mae could mentally wander any further down the panic path.

"Yes, yes. That's actually not what I brought you in to talk about—although of course we do look forward to you meeting that deadline." Elizabeth took a beat to rearrange her hands. Mae's watch beeped in encouragement and she slapped her wrist to cover it. She could feel sweat building on her brow and tried to dash it away with a subtle hair fluff. After a dramatic pause Elizabeth resumed. "Obviously I wanted to introduce myself but I also thought, 'tis the season for some friendly advice, no?"

"We always appreciate feedback," charmed Neal as Mae used all her energy to stop her eyes from going into a wild roll.

"Great!" exclaimed Elizabeth. "And I always appreciate people who appreciate feedback." Mae's left brow started to twitch as Elizabeth locked her in a stare and continued. "Mae, I know your Laela won *Best New Detective* for your first book. And, I know that many people love it, but we can always be better. SO! I do think the tone of your books, they're sort of, shall we say, atypical. It might do you well to mature your character a little this time around. It's a dignified genre. Read some classics. Brainstorm. How can Laela grow?! Maybe you could do a writing retreat?"

"A writing retreat," Mae repeated. It felt like her ears were turning red from the built-up pressure of not losing her mind.

"Well!" Neal stepped in, likely sensing the radiating heat. "Mae was in fact just telling me that she's planning to go to New Hampshire to write in the woods for the rest of the month."

Before Mae could mention that she was actually moving there Elizabeth piped in, delighted, "The woods! How Thoreau. I love it!"

"Well, it's more…" Mae was committed to being completely above board. It was another one of her punishing habits.

"It's so much more quiet than the city," said Neal, taking Mae's sentence in a different direction entirely. He shot Mae a glance letting her know that all the details need not be shared at this exact moment. Mae then shot Neal a glance back letting him know that this whole situation was giving her a rash.

"Good! Then we're all on the same page." Elizabeth laughed. "Same PAGE!" Mae's eyes bulged with words unspoken. "Thank you for coming in," Elizabeth said as she stood up, making it clear that she was finished. "I look forward to your new and improved next book."

Mae and Neal stood. Mae sensed that the twitch in her brow was about to take over the entire left side of her face if she didn't say something in her defense. But, instead, Mae bit down on her lip. Knowing from her sorted history of experiences that she would do far better if she just waited a few minutes and made sure that what she wanted to say would be best conveyed by the words that came out of her mouth.

"We'll be getting in touch soon then," said Neal, as they walked out of the office door into the hall. "Thank you."

Mae, still not trusting herself to open her mouth, did a friendly goodbye gesture. The editor responded with what looked like the Queen's wave. Neal ushered Mae down the hall.

"What was that?!" Mae aggressively whispered as they hot footed it towards the door.

"Let's wait until we're at the elevator bank," responded Neal, trying to keep a lid on the whole the situation.

"More mature? Are you KIDDING me?!" Mae didn't like lids.

"Elevator. Elevator. Elevate…. Oh, bye, Steven." Neal stopped his elevator mantra as they passed the reception desk.

"Mae Robards. Neal Michaels." Steven stood up. "Thank you for coming by. Happy Holidays."

Mae stopped her dramatic plank walk to address Steven properly. "Thank you, Steven. And a very Happy Holiday Season to you as well." Neal put a gentle hand on Mae's shoulder maneuvering her towards the outer door before she said anything else.

"Read the classics?!" Mae burst out when they finally reached the elevators. "Like I haven't. Could she be anymore condescending?! And EMOTIONALLY DISHEVELED. Give me a break." Mae was fully prepared to go on for days. She was riled.

"She probably just felt like she had to say something, to have some criticism, establish herself as the new head editor." Neal was forever looking for a middle ground.

"Nope. Gross. Rude." She was not a fan of middle grounds at all. "Let a male detective be *emotionally disheveled* and he's marching to his own beat—he's idiosyncratic! But a LADY detective who is perhaps a tad all over the place, well, she's just a real mess! She should mature, straighten out, get it together. Well, I don't think so! What year is this? Oh, and I just loved the *How Thoreau* comment. I'm sure she finds rural life to be *so quaint*. I can't!" Mae took a pause to breathe and give her fingers a break from all the air quotes. Then she started right back up again. "And I do not like how we glossed over that I'm actually moving to New Hampshire, Neal, it feels dishonest."

"It's not dishonest," Neal stated firmly. "It's picking and choosing which part of the information to lead with."

"Hmmmmmm…" Mae shook her head. "So, finessing?"

"Yes. Finessing." Neal smiled.

"Sounds like a lot dishonesty!" Even though Mae was worked up she managed a laugh. What else could she do at this point?! "What *was* that, Neal? She wants my voice to be more mature? I'm an adult woman."

"I'll follow up with her for more specifics. In the meantime, why don't we just stick with the original plan of you finishing up your draft, in your voice, the way you want. Forget about what she said for right now, OK? We'll deal with it later, you have enough on your plate." Neal said, always the pragmatist.

"Great." Mae responded, feeling not so very great at all. "I'll just move my entire life across the country, figure out how to float the ski enter until I have the time to help my parents restructure, finish the novel, and on top of it all, I'll just pretend I didn't hear that the new head editor said I should make changes to my lead character!" Mae loved a run on sentence. "And, all in three weeks!"

"Yes," replied Neal as if Mae wasn't being facetious. He looked down at his watch to double check the date. "Actually, you have exactly twenty-two days until the book is due. Twenty-three if you count today. Seems much better than only three weeks, doesn't it?! And, knowing you, I'm sure you've started packing already." Neal smiled broadly. This was his way of being supportive, of putting on a good face, to show it all could get done. "It's like you always tell me Mae, Christmas is a time for miracles." The elevator dinged.

Chapter 3 - The Ubiquitous Christmas Coffee

*M*ae arrived at the coffee shop a few minutes early. As she glanced out at the patio seating area, she noticed that her friend Julie was already there. Mae waved and pointed to the counter signaling that she would grab a coffee and be right out.

It had been one of the great miracles of Mae's life that she'd met Julie her very first week of living in Los Angeles. She'd been in the park writing, when one of the many notes she'd stuck all over her laptop had blown away and landed smack dab on Julie's face. Mae had jumped up in apology as Julie laughed and walked over to return the flying piece of paper.

They'd become instant friends, and, as Mae's writing had begun to take off over the years so had Julie's directing career. Mae had always been in awe of her friend's confident and decisive intelligence. She was incredibly grateful to know Julie, who was forever making her laugh with her dry humor and constant assertions that Mae should learn to meditate (which they both knew was never going to happen). Mae was even out with Julie the night that she'd first met her now wife, Sarah Jackson. The two friends had been through so many life events together over the years that now, as Mae was faced with the moment of telling Julie about her decision to move, she felt so incredibly sad. Mae picked up her coffee order and headed out to the patio. She was so lost in going over the right words to say that she stumbled over a woman's chair on the path to Julie.

"Oh, my goodness, I am SO sorry!" Mae immediately gushed to the woman as she righted herself and tried to wipe off the coffee that she'd spilled down her own jacket. She would've been completely mortified if she wasn't so used to it. When Mae finally arrived at Julie's table she shrugged, "Who lets me out of the house?!"

"I do love me a little *Maeeee-ham*." Julie winked at the inside joke that had become a constant callback. "Just say your moon is in the wrong house, everyone here will understand," she said as she winked again, her eyes full of friendly laughter. "Good thing you always wear black so no one will notice." Julie was forever teasing Mae about her New York City commitment to dark colors.

Mae laughed as she took off her black belted trench. The jacket, she thought, was very much like the kind of detective-y type coat her main character, Laela, would wear. They had heat lamps out on the patio, and although everyone else in LA thought it was cold, Mae had never quite acclimated to how mild the winters were there. In fact, Mae wouldn't even call it winter because she always associated the season with snow.

As Mae hung her coat on the back of the chair, she accidentally knocked her remaining coffee onto the ground. Mae quickly picked up the cup, thankfully the *to-go* lid had remained on during the fall, and looked around. "I'm so sorry. I must be retrograding!" Mae exclaimed to no one in particular, not even really sure if a person could retrograde.

"This is a lot of spilling, even for you," Julie smiled. "You must have a huge decision coming up!"

"What?" It was like her friend knew that Mae had something important to tell her.

"You always get rattled when you have a big choice to make," stated Julie.

"Jeez! Jules, you know me too well," Mae admitted.

"SO…" Julie prodded.

"So," Mae took a deep breath. "Two things…"

"TWO things!" repeated Julie as she scooted her chair in closer, getting ready for whatever Mae had to tell her.

31

"Yeah, well, the first is a random sort of out of nowhere thing."

"Warming up for the big one then?" Julie posited correctly.

"Yeah, I guess," admitted Mae. "I just came from a meeting with the new head editor at my publishers, who said that I needed to *mature* my voice. Or that my main character's voice needs to *mature* at least." Mae was back to using air quotes for the words she found insulting.

"WHAT?!" Julie jumped, not liking this update in the least bit. "Did you mention that your main character's voice is why people like YOUR writing so much!" Julie was such a good and supportive friend.

"I didn't know what to say in the moment," admitted Mae. "And I felt like the things that would've come out of my mouth at the time probably wouldn't have been appropriate, so… I guess I also felt guilty because I am so behind schedule."

"Mae. It's YOUR voice!" Julie stated firmly.

"Well, I know," said Mae, so grateful that her friend always had her back. "But it is true that I'm not a standard structured novelist."

"Who wants standard?!" Julie responded in a manner which made it clear that she most certainly did not.

"Apparently a lot of people," shrugged Mae. "Or at least Elizabeth Birk does." They both sat for a second, thinking. Neither of them were standard people. But who was really? No one Mae knew, that was for sure.

"So, what's the second thing?" asked Julie.

"Ummm, ok so…" Mae dragged out the words.

"Just spill it," Julie cut in.

"My parents were going to sell the cross country ski center…" Mae began, now fully committed to getting it all out on the table as quickly as possible. "It's too much for them to continue to maintain without more help, which they don't at the moment have the finances for… So. Anyways. They called to tell me this on Sunday. And… and I decided I would move home and help them run it." Mae had gotten all the words out at last. Telling her best friend had finally made it all real and Mae felt suddenly like she wanted to cry.

"You're serious," Julie stated gently.

"Yeah, I'm serious. I've thought about it really hard Jules. I even laid on the floor and watched ALL THREE *Lord of the Rings*—that always helps me clear my head!"

Mae admitted to her friend. But, of course, Julie already knew this about her.

"So, you brought out the big guns," Julie smiled.

"Extended edition I'm assuming."

"Of course," replied Mae in all her earnest nerdiness.

"Of course. It IS a huge decision." A response Julie meant as a kind jest about her friend's continued use of *Lord of the Rings* as some kind of a coping mechanism. It was a quality that the two friends did not share at all but one that Julie seemed to find to be delightfully special about Mae.

"I'm sorry that I waited to tell you." Mae had felt bad about that. "I just wanted to say it in person, not on the phone."

"I understand," whispered Julie. And, of course, Mae knew that she truly did understand. It just felt sad.

"I've been going over and over it in my mind. It just feels right." Mae was still sure, well at least mostly sure, that she was making the right decision.

"Do you need any help packing?" Julie asked as her eyes teared up a little. Julie would not tell her friend to stay. That was not the kind of relationship they had. But they would miss each other, they would miss each other so very much.

"Thank you, Julie." Mae reached across the table and took her hand. "Thank you for being my friend and for going along on this insane journey with me. I've been so stuck on my book. Three extensions! You know that's never happened to me before. And, I'm so afraid that I won't be able to find my rhythm again. When my parents called, something just went off in my brain… I want to be closer while I still have them in my life. I think it's making me restless. Anyways, I just have to go with my gut on this one and try to trust that it will turn out OK… Even though I know I'm not really good at doing that." Mae grimaced.

"Maybe this is exactly what you need Mae!" Julie said, clearly committed to supporting her friend's decision with as much confidence as she had in her. "A big change to spark your imagination!"

"You're too good to me, Jules," warmed Mae. She so desperately needed to hear the words of encouragement.

"What is this?" Julie brightened. "The beginning of a Christmas movie? Big city girl moves back home to save the family business."

"Julie!" Mae laughed. "Well," Mae started, entirely too familiar with all the lovable tropes of the genre she enjoyed so very much. "We do already have the drinking coffee part down. There's always SUCH a tremendous amount of coffee drinking in those movies!"

"Well, we definitely have coffee EVERYWHERE!" Julie said as she pointed at Mae's jacket.

"So now all we need is a kind stranger, some cookie baking montages, snow, a misunderstanding, and a kiss that doesn't happen until the very end. I mean, I'll be staying with my parents, so I don't think I'll be kissing any boys." Mae made a face.

"Mae!" Julie laughed. "Let's be honest, it's not like you're kissing any boys now."

"SO hurtful!" Mae feigned shock. "But also, oooooh so true." At that moment Mae couldn't even remember when she'd last had a proper kiss. Like a really good one, the kind of kiss that shot straight to your toes, hitting all the good parts on the way down.

"Of course, as the leading lady you'll have to wear a red jacket," Julie pointed out.

"Always with the red jacket in these Christmas movies!" Mae agreed enthusiastically. "But they're never actually dressed for a proper winter, did you notice?"

"That's such a New Hampshire thing to say." Julie laughed.

"It's true! Look for it when you're watching all the Christmas romance movies this year. Almost NO ONE has appropriate winter socks on!" Mae was adamant. And she knew what she was talking about, she had watched nearly every holiday flick available. The movies always delighted Mae and she found comfort in their promised happy endings. We could all do with a little bit of that, Mae thought.

"You're an insane person, looking at socks." Julie brought her back to the moment. "Are you going to fly back?"

"No, I'm gonna drive," Mae responded. "I think the Jeep has at least one big cross country trip left in her." Mae smiled bittersweetly at her friend. She hoped that she had at least one left in her, too.

The Holiday Breakdown

Chapter 4 - The Cross Country Sendoff

A week and a half later, very, very early on Saturday morning, Mae was out front of her (soon to be ex) apartment building trying to shove one last box into her 1986 red Jeep Cherokee. The vehicle had been given to her when her grandfather passed on so what it lacked in modern advances it made up for in heart.

The past eleven days had been a real whirlwind. Mae couldn't believe that she had packed up an entire life in less than two weeks. There had been calls to make, addresses to change, goodbyes to be said, and every night Mae had continued to write. The story structure was there, the actual mystery plot was there, but something was still missing and Mae couldn't put her finger on it.

As Neal had surmised, Mae had immediately begun packing the moment she'd told her parents that she was coming home to help. But things really started getting done after her coffee date with Julie when her friend had come back to the apartment, and together they began to plow through everything. Julie's wife, Sarah, had also come over later that evening with extra cleaning supplies and boxes. Mae's friends had helped her do a trips

Goodwill for drop-off and had even continued packing Mae's stuff when she went out to run final errands. Mae felt so incredibly lucky, and so loved. She couldn't really think about how much she was going to miss them because it would just shake her to the core. Instead, she focused on committing to seeing their faces as much as possible. Mae had gotten everyone matching (paper) calendars so they could coordinate calls and she also decided that there would be scheduled trips back and forth for the friends to catch up in person.

Shortly after Mae had told Julie and Sarah about the move, she'd reached out to her close childhood friend, Renee Donato, back in New Hampshire to let her she was coming. Mae had also spent some time on the phone with her parents outlining what had to happen with the ski center. It really all boiled down to physical help, they just needed an extra set of hands and a tad more business. Obviously, without a tad more business, they couldn't afford a tad more help, which is where Mae would step in. And, since she was no longer going to be paying rent in Los Angeles, she could just flip that money over to the center; hopefully giving them enough padding to make it a few months while she got everything together. Well, that was as long as she got her draft in on time and Peterson's didn't take the advance back. Mae did not want to even think about the possibility of that happening. But, of course, she thought about it anyway, over and over again, all the way up until moving day.

When Mae finally got the trunk of her Jeep closed it looked as if it might burst. She turned to Julie and Sarah who were standing on the sidewalk with Scarpetta at their feet. They had decided that Mae would leave at dawn to give her as much daylight driving time as possible, and so that they could watch one more West Coast sunrise together. The friends, all bundled up for the cold(ish) desert December morning weather, held hands as rays of light shot out over the sky and lit up the beautiful palm trees. Pinks, peaches, blues, yellows. It was incredible! Mae remembered back to when she saw her first sunset in LA, it was one of her most favorite memories. She'd never been on the West Coast before and was in absolute awe at how the sun just went over, falling off into a vast ocean of orange fire. Mae told herself that there would be more sunset and sunrise visits in the future. She just couldn't stand to think about it as her *last* anything, otherwise she wouldn't be able to get into the Jeep and drive away. Mae reminded herself, that no matter what, she would always have these moments to look back on.

"OK. This is it," Mae turned to her friends. "Here we go!"

"This is so exciting, Mae. You are on a new adventure!" Sarah exclaimed. Sarah was probably the most positive person Mae had ever known in her life and she was so deeply pleased that Julie and Sarah had found each other. The two had met at a party for a film Julie was directing. Sarah had been the audio engineer for another one of the film producer's projects. Mae had been standing with her amazing director friend waiting for the passed appetizers to come by when Sarah had walked over and introduced herself. The two had hit it off immediately and started dating. Sarah brought so much joy and enthusiasm with her wherever she went, it had knocked Julie right off her feet.

"I just want to state, for the record… or for myself really." This was something that had been growing in the back of Mae's mind and she needed to say it out loud to her friends. "That just because I'm moving back to where I started, that doesn't mean that *I'm* going backwards. I just… I just want to make the most of the time I have with my parents. And, I want them to have

the ski center for as long as they want. And, and...
maybe I need to be *there* in order to move forward, with
my writing, I mean." Mae felt like her fragilities were
poised to start running over.

"Mae," Julie stepped in. "It's BECAUSE you
followed your dreams here to become a writer that
you're now in the position to be able move to New
Hampshire and help out your family. It's going to work
out." Julie stepped closer to Mae and wrapped her in a
big hug.

"It IS working out!" Sarah stated with happy,
manifesting words. She joined in the group hug and the
three took a moment to just be there, together, in the
breaking dawn.

"You're such good friends," Mae gushed as she
forced herself out of the warm hug and towards her Jeep.
"OK! Scarpetta, get in the car booboo!" Mae opened the
backdoor and her pooch jumped in. Then Mae willed
herself to walk around to the front driver's side.

"Keep us posted Mae!" cheered Sarah.

"We look forward to hearing all about some high
school love who you bump into and rekindle the old
flame." Julie, keeping the mood up.

"Jules!" Mae exclaimed, fake exasperated. "This is not a Christmas romance story!" The idea gave her enough of a good enough laugh to propel Mae into the Jeep and turn on the ignition. Mae glanced in her mirror just in time to see Julie raise an eyebrow, as if saying that she clearly knew a holiday romance set up when she saw one.

Chapter 5 - The Breakdown I

*M*ae's cross country strategy was to drive south of Colorado; it added a few hours but she didn't want to risk any wild weather. She'd go through Arizona, New Mexico, Texas and then start heading north at Oklahoma. Mae planned to stop at roadside motels when she needed to sleep and to stare at her manuscript. She thought that the time in the car would give her mind the space it needed to come up with what was missing from her book. At least, that was what she hoped.

So, Mae drove. And she drove. She sang along to holiday songs on the radio to help keep her spirits up and her eyes open. Time passed as Mae belted out her favorite carols. About every hour or so she would break it up by making eye contact with Scarpetta in the rearview and exclaim, "Mature my voice! Are you kidding me?!" The words of Elizabeth Birk popping back into her head. Usually, Mae would follow that up with an exasperated, "What am I even doing?!" Scarpetta didn't seem to have any answers either but she always looked like she wanted to help. And so, the two faithful friends drove on.

The Holiday Breakdown

Mae had been making good time and was still managing to get a little writing done in the wee small hours of the morning. She would push straight through long days of driving (pulling over for gas, snacks and doggie breaks), and stop at night to walk Scarpetta, get dinner, write, and sleep. Then she would rise very early, get extra coffee, walk the pooch, and start the process again.

On Monday, Mae was about ten hours in on her third full day of driving. She was somewhere just southeast of Louisville when she decided to pull off the highway and look for a hotel. As Mae drove down a smaller Kentucky road in search of a place to stay for the night the engine light suddenly flashed bright red on the dash. The Jeep immediately started making a loud clunk, clunk, clunkity clunk sound. Mae, whose parents had forced her to take a defensive driving course when she first got her license, masterfully pulled to the side of the bumpy road and eased on the brakes. The engine clunked its last clunk and then went dead.

"Dang it!" Mae let out the adrenaline filled words. She leaned over the seat to give Scarpetta a head scratch and make sure she was alright. Mae was very grateful that they'd made it safely off the road. She tried the key in the ignition. Nothing. She breathed deeply and pulled out her phone. No point in freaking out completely, she told herself. She'd just handle the situation and then freak out later. Mae called her insurance, who said they'd notify the nearest open garage for a tow. Then she called her mother, who after making sure Mae was okay, let her know that she should have had the old Jeep checked before driving cross country. Mae claimed that she had to go and hung up the phone before she said something she didn't mean.

"Mom and I will probably murder each other before I can even finish my book." She told Scarpetta, who had come up to the front seat now that they weren't moving. "Which actually might not be that bad since I can't seem to finish anyways... Mom thinks I should've taken the Jeep to a mechanic before I left. Ridiculous! I was SO busy!" Mae looked to her dog for backup but Scarpetta gave her a look in return which seemed to suggest that she was on Mae's mom's side. "OK, fine. You're both probably right!" Mae shrugged, mad at herself. Then Mae threw out another, "What am I even doing?!" just for good measure.

Mae was looking out into the beautiful twilight dusted landscape for answers when a tow truck came rambling towards them and pulled a u-ey to edge in behind Mae. The door of the truck opened and out stepped a man who immediately made Mae feel as if her seat heaters were on. Mae's Jeep didn't have seat heaters, but she checked anyway. It was suddenly so hot inside that she had to roll down the window, physically, because her Jeep was that old—she obviously should have had it checked out before she left. Mae mentally kicked herself again, it was lucky the wheels had stayed on. Well, I can't go back in time, Mae thought, as she did what she hoped looked like a casual wave out the now open window. The figure walking towards her waved back in the fading December light. Of course, Mae pondered, breakdowns could have their good points.

"Hollllllllly smokes," Mae breathed to Scarpetta as she eyed the approaching man. "Maybe this is a Christmas romance story." He came up to her window and leaned in, gifting Mae with a perfect view of the most beautiful brown eyes she'd ever seen in her entire life. Jingle. Bells.

"Hey, I'm Jack Wilder. Did you call for a tow?" Jack asked as he pushed up the sleeves to his jacket.

"It wasn't me!" Mae responded with a smile after a brief pause of being momentarily and utterly frozen. Was she flirting? She didn't know why she'd just said that but it was most likely the forearms. She was going to have to beat her head against a wall as soon as the vehicle was fixed.

"It must have been you then," Jack said to Scarpetta. Mae laughed, which was all she had left in her arsenal. Jack stepped back as Mae opened the door to climb out. Scarpetta bound down behind her and ran over to Jack for a sniff. Fortunate girl, Mae thought.

"I'm Mae Robards. And this is Scarpetta." Mae introduced as her dog unapologetically dropped to the ground hoping for a rub. "She really loves a good belly scratch." Mae gave Scarpetta an eyeball. Scarpetta looked back at her brazenly.

"Scarpetta, huh? Where are you two headed?" Jack asked as he gladly obliged the pooch with a good rubdown.

"It's from a crime series I love by Patricia Cornwell. Kay Scarpetta is the lead character; she's a medical examiner. Anyways…" Too much information, Mae thought as she cut herself off. "We are driving cross country. LA to New Hampshire."

"Well, Mae and Scarpetta, let's get you loaded up so we can see what's happening with your vehicle and have you back on the road in time for Christmas." Jack stood up and dusted off his pants.

Mae's eyes lingered a little too long on the freshly dusted leg area and she became further appalled at herself. She never acted like this! And now was most certainly not an appropriate occasion to start. She had a book to finish, a ski center to run, and now a Jeep to fix! It was definitely not the time to be looking at men's pants. She had to pull it together, but not before she got one quick glimpse of Jack's toosh as he walked back towards his truck. Wow! She immediately wanted to call Julie. It was *that* good of a bum. It was phone-a-friend worthy. Mae's cheeks suddenly turned almost as red as her Jeep. She looked around anxiously feeling as if someone had seen her blush and decided that it was probably just Scarpetta reading her thoughts. Mae must have been in the car too long, she told herself. That was why her brain was acting up. It could happen to anyone! She was just tired, or hungry, or any one of a myriad of things. But what she most certainly was not was a giddy teenager. How disgraceful!

"Sounds good," Mae managed after what felt like a little too long of a delay in response.

"So, your insurance contacted us because we're the closet open garage. I assume they messaged you with the details as well, but just to confirm... I'll be taking you to Rex's in Warbler Cross. Rex Johnson is the owner. He's an honest man and will do right by you guys," Jack explained. "If you were going to breakdown, this is the place to do it."

"Oh, that's good to know. I'm glad I at least planned that part well." Mae didn't care what people often said about sarcasm being the lowest form of humor, it always made her feel better, and she figured that people who didn't enjoy it were probably no fun anyway. Jack laughed a gorgeous laugh and smiled at Mae which instantly triggered a choir singing a round of *The Hallelujah Chorus* in her head. "Are you also a mechanic or is your specialty people in distress?" Mae winced inwardly and wished that she would stop saying such silly things but they just seemed to keep slipping out of her mouth.

"Actually," Jacked laughed again. "I'm a Ranger with the Forest Service. I was working nearby, but..." He seemed to be choosing his words carefully. "This is a down time right now so I've been... I'm helping Rex out for the time being." Mae nodded her head, sort of understanding.

With the Jeep loaded up onto the bed, Jack opened the passenger door for Mae to climb into the cab of the truck. She scrambled in and Jack handed the pooch up to Mae, as it was just a little too high for her to jump. Mae nudged Scarpetta to go sit in between herself and the driver's seat because setting up a perimeter seemed like the safest thing to do. As Jack got in, Mae eyed some Christmas tinsel that was hanging from the mirror. How apropos, she thought as the truck rumbled to a start.

Chapter 6 - The Kindness of Strangers

*M*ae stood inside the carport watching as Rex Johnson talked to himself under the hood of her Jeep. He had come out to greet them right as they'd pulled around back of the small garage. Mae had liked him instantly. Rex came across as a man who loved his work and was proud of his small business. It reminded her of her parents, which had the immediate effect of relaxing Mae, making her feel at home and in capable hands. Also, Mae tended to trust people who talked to themselves (obviously there were some exceptions). But, in general, since she did it so much, she had to assume that anyone caught talking to themselves was probably in the midst of perfecting their art. Mae was hoping that Rex's art was fixing old Jeeps.

As Mae threw out wishes to the Universe that whatever was wrong with her vehicle would be easily manageable, the door behind her opened and Jack emerged from a back office. An absolutely adorable scruffy pup with a short brownish coat and lankly limbs bounded out alongside him but came skidding to a stop upon seeing they had guests. Jack bent down and gave the little cutie a calming scratch.

"This is my guy, Sammy. He's still a bit shy. We found him on the side of the road a few months back, no tags. We put up posters but no one came to claim him so I took him home," explained Jack. Mae felt so sorry for the pup who'd been abandoned, and also, totally enamored by the man who clearly had such a soft heart. You lucky, lucky dog, Mae thought as her mouth went suddenly dry.

"Sammy did you say?" Mae asked, hoping that the question sounded normal and not as if there was a flash desert happening in her throat. Mae tried to subtly wet her lips and pull her tongue of the roof of her mouth. Pull yourself together Mae, she thought.

"Yeah, Sammy. His full name is Samwise, from *The Lord of the Rings,* arguably the cornerstone character of the trilogy." Jack looked at her questioningly, as if wondering if she was familiar with THE trilogy.

"Arguably." That was all Mae could get out. She was overwhelmed. The man was a ten-alarm fire, loved dogs, AND *Lord of the Rings*. She couldn't take it. Her lips were now completely stuck to her teeth. She tried to casually swallow in an effort to get moisture going again and turned her attention to Scarpetta who was slowly moving toward Sammy.

Jack followed her gaze over to the dogs to see what was transpiring. "It's OK boy," he urged. "This is Mae and Scarpetta." The two dogs eyeballed each other in a getting to know you type of dance, but the pup meet and greet was quickly interrupted by the sound of Rex closing the hood of the Jeep.

"What's it looking like?" Mae asked nervously.

"It's the carburetor," said Rex as he wiped his hands on a rag. "It's an easy fix but I'm going to have to order the part. I can place the request tonight but I'm guessing it won't get processed until tomorrow morning. We can probably have y'all out of here in two days."

"Two days!" exclaimed Mae. She'd secretly been hoping that they would be on the road again tomorrow morning.

"I'm sorry about that, but it's the best I can do." Rex replied earnestly. "I don't keep this kind of part in stock. This is an older, shall we say more classic, vehicle. Newer Jeeps don't even use these types of carburetors anymore."

"Of course, of course!" Mae jumped in quickly. "I'm just mad at myself for not getting it checked before I left. I really appreciate your help."

"My pleasure ma'am!" Rex said as he and Mae shook hands. Mae normally hated being called *ma'am*. She even had a term for it; she referred to as a *sneak attack ma'am-ing*. An example of which would be if Mae was out and about, feeling good, and a stranger walking by would all of a sudden (and totally unprovoked), say, *Have a great day... MA'AM.* It made her feel like she had to go home, put on more under eye make-up and start the entire day over again. Ma'am?! Was she ninety? Did she look like she needed help figuring out what emojis meant? The exceptions to sneak attack Ma'aming were of course if it was someone from the south or if someone was in the military. At which point Mae just took it as a very polite address, and the situation went from appalling to endearing. Like in this circumstance.

"Well," Jack jumped in. "Maybe this is a great opportunity to explore a little piece of America you would have otherwise missed." He smiled again at Mae and it felt like Christmas lights were suddenly blazing in her head and she thought she heard the Whos in Whoville singing.

"Why don't you take them over to Mitzey's Motel?" Rex suggested to Jack and then moved his focus back to Mae. "Mitzey Hernandez is the proprietor. She'll give you a real great deal. Plus, Mitzey makes the best breakfast in the entire state of Kentucky. Maybe even in the entire country!"

"I don't want to be any trouble. If it's easier to just give me directions... Scarpetta and I will walk or take a cab or whatever." Mae looked over at the Jeep with all of her stuff crammed in.

"It's no trouble at all," Jack smiled. "Mitzey's is right across the street. Here, let me help you with some of your bags and I'll take you over and introduce everyone."

Mae popped the trunk, quickly grabbing any renegade boxes that tried to escape. She took the bag she had for Scarpetta and the night suitcase she'd been taking into hotels for herself which had all her toiletries, her workout clothes, pjs, an extra change of clothes, and probably twenty pair of panties and socks which to some may seem ridiculous but one never knew what was going to happen. Best to always have backup panties, say for example, if you got stuck in Kentucky for a few days. And, Mae always had extra socks, even in her regular day bag. Wet feet could take a girl down. She was already wearing her heavier jacket, which she'd put on when they were waiting for the tow, so she rummaged through the back looking for her scarf. While searching for warmer gear she happened to come across the bag with her favorite onesie that flattered her figure and made her look like a cool pilot on a starship. She called a mental audible and grabbed that bag as well, just in case. Then Mae went around front for her computer and day backpack. She peered into the Jeep at everything she'd be leaving and, for a brief moment, questioned if she should bring it all in.

"I lock up at night and live over the garage," Rex said as if reading Mae's mind. "Everything will be fine." Mae had become much more safety conscious after living in the city for so long, but she still remembered what small towns where like. Plus, she had a good feeling about Rex and for some reason felt totally comfortable leaving all her worldly goods with a person she'd just met. Also, she was just too dang tired to carry it all inside.

"Thank you," said Mae as she closed the door and tossed Rex her keys.

"Come on, I'll take you to Mitzey's," Jack said to Mae. He turned to Rex, "I'll be back to help you lock up and to grab Sammy." Jack gave his pup a pat, picked up Mae's suitcase and then headed towards the front door.

Mae, Jack and Scarpetta ventured out onto the street. Mae hadn't really gotten a good look at Warbler Cross when they'd first driven in; she had been too occupied ogling the driver. Now that she had a moment to take in the area, she was struck by how beautiful it was. They were standing on a classic main thoroughfare with all the store fronts sitting close to the road. Off to her left, she could see the Warbler Cross Town Common with a gazebo decorated in full holiday cheer. It was getting very dark but lamp posts lit up the town and illuminated the lush green wreaths and red bows that delicately dressed the street. Mae wrapped her scarf around her neck and watched her breath crystalize when it hit the chilly crisp December air. It was like a classical Christmas town, she thought!

Jack led the way, pointing towards a cute two-story building that was literally across the street from the garage. It had an adorable little porch over which *Mitzey's Motel* was painted on the awning. When they got closer Mae could read a smaller sign just above the door that read *Dogs Welcome*. Mae smiled at Scarpetta as they stepped inside. It *did* seem like a very lovey place for a breakdown, if a person *had* to have one.

Jack led Mae and Scarpetta into the warm lobby. She looked around to see a beautifully decorated tree, little white lights strung along the ceiling rafters and there was even a gorgeous fire burning in the fireplace. Mae thought that as far as cute picture-perfect Christmases scenes went, Mitzey's really nailed it. The room even smelled of the holidays.

A woman came out from the back smiling. "Jack!" she exclaimed. Mae assumed that this must be Mitzey as she seemed to match the feel of the place perfectly. Joyous, bright and warm.

"Hey Mitzey! I brought you some guests. This is Mae and Scarpetta."

Mae nodded hello and stepped to the check-in desk where she noticed a gorgeous plate of homemade cookies set out on red doilies. She was indeed in a Christmas town! "Your place is absolutely perfect." Mae gushed. "It looks like a Hallmark movie."

"Why thank you!" Mitzey beamed. "I saw you being towed into Rex's and figured that you might be coming over. And, it so happens, that I JUST baked a fresh batch of Doggie Trees." She reached under the desk and pulled out a plate of what seemed to be cookies shaped like Christmas trees, only they were very thick and super chunky. There was a note on the plate in the shape of a puppy with all the ingredients handwritten on it. "We like to keep ALL our guests happy," said Mitzey as she picked up one of the treats. "May I?"

Mae looked at Scarpetta, whose tail was up in full wag. Clearly, she knew what was about to go down. "I think Scarpetta would never forgive me if I denied her a Doggie Tree."

"Scarpetta? After the amazing Scarpetta in the Patricia Cornwell series?" Mitzey asked.

"The very one!" Mae responded absolutely delighted to meet a fellow Cornwell buff. "I'm a huge fan!"

"I'm a bit of a thriller lady myself!" Mitzey said, as she pointed towards the other end of the lobby. Along a wall adjacent to the hearth stood a huge bookcase packed full. "I like to keep them out for my guests to enjoy." Mitzey took a beat then refocused her attention. "Here I am going on when you must be so tired! Let's get you set up. Welcome to Mitzey's Motel! It's more of an inn than a motel really, but I do love the alliteration."

"Of course!" Mae agreed.

"I'm a pretty big puns guy myself," added Jack.

"Oh no!" Mae laughed.

"Oh yes," Jack responded very seriously. And then all three of them started laughing. Mae caught herself so full of giggles that she tried to shake it off. She was giddy teenager-ing again. This was getting a little ridiculous, she thought.

"Well! If you wouldn't mind giving me your John Hancock right here on the registry, please?" Mitzey turned the sign-in book towards Mae and handed her a pen. "Breakfast is from 7am to 9am. I try to do a mix so there's something for everyone."

"Oh, I've heard about your amazing breakfasts!" Mae was very much looking forward to it in fact.

"A lady does like to be proud of her pancakes," said Mitzey nobly. "You are in room 203. It's just up the stairs and to the left."

Mae handed Mitzey the signed registry. "Thank you, I…"

Mitzey, who had been about to hand Mae her keys, looked down at the registry and then excitedly cut in. "Mae Robards? Mae Robards the author?"

"Well I…" Mae felt herself blushing.

Mitzey took off like a shot across the lobby and headed straight to the bookshelf. She fumbled through well-loved paperbacks until she came across one in particular: *Finding Laela*. Mitzey pulled it out and flipped it open to look inside the back cover at the picture of Mae. "I knew I recognized you! You got the *Watson's Winner Award* for *Best New Detective* a few years back when you introduced the series. You're the author of the Laela Sarno novels! I love them!"

"I... Thank you so much!" Mae's blush deepened.

"Her main character's name is Laela and she's sort of an accidental detective," Mitzey explained to Jack. "In the first book she gets set up for a crime and then no one believes she didn't do it. And then... well maybe I shouldn't tell you so you can read them yourself."

Mae felt embarrassed but also completely delighted. This pleased her to the core. It was so wonderful to meet a fan of her books.

"I really appreciate it," beamed Mae.

"I've plowed through all four!" Mitzey said excitedly. "That Detective Williams, he seems like a real upstanding and handsome guy! Of course, so does Laela's partner PI Lin. But they have a solid working friendship as far as I can tell... I'll stop. I don't mean to keep you. I'm just so excited to have a real author in my motel. Maybe, before you leave, we could take a picture and you'd be willing to sign one of my books?"

63

"Oh, of course, absolutely!" Mae gushed. "It would be my pleasure."

Mitzey returned the book to the shelf and handed Mae the keys she'd been clutching.

"Well, Ms. Finding Laela," Jack said as he gave Mae the suitcase he was still holding. "It's been a pleasure meeting you. I have to head back to Rex's. We'll most likely have more information about your Jeep tomorrow morning if you want to stop by." He nodded his handsome head toward the ladies. "Mae. Mitzey. Scarpetta." The ladies nodded in return and watched as Jack headed for the door.

"Thanks again, Jack!" Mae added as she watched Jack's fine form exit the motel. Someone had said their prayers, she thought.

"Jack looks a little bit like the description of your Detective Williams, wouldn't you say?" Mitzey asked in a tone which Mae would almost consider to be conspiratorial.

"What? I hadn't thought about it…" Mae blushed again. It was true that Detective Williams and Jack had many similar physical qualities. And mayyyyyybe, Mae admitted to herself, the description was one she found to be exceedingly attractive. Mae further reddened. That was multiple blushes in a very short period of time. What a day it was turning out to be, she thought!

"We have a *Lite Bites* evening menu that's available for another two hours if you're hungry." Mitzey's words broke Mae out of her scarlet bloom. "What else did I forget to tell you? Oh! The Wi-Fi password is *Marple*."

"Wonderful!" Mae smiled at the reference and Mitzey's love of mysteries which seemed to match her own. "Thanks so much, Mitzey. You've really brightened my day." Mae picked up her other bags and headed for the stairs. Scarpetta gave one longing last look at where the Doggie Trees had come from and then darted up behind her.

Mae opened door number 203 to find a perfectly tidy room with all the necessities. A wreath hung over the dresser and Christmas decorations adorned the windows. It was so pretty, Mae thought, as she threw the bags down on the floor and immediately reached for her phone to FaceTime Julie.

"Mae!" Julie picked up on second ring. Mae could see that her friends were in the kitchen, apparently baking. "We got your text about the Jeep. So glad you called. Fill us in! What happened?"

"I don't even know where to start Julie. Oh, my goodness, this day has been WILD!" Mae was walking around her cute temporary quarters, checking out the little Christmas details Mitzey had added all over the room. "Quick side note, how adorable is this room? And, are you two baking right now?"

"Very adorable," responded Julie as Mae flipped the phone around to show her the entire set up. "And yeah, Sarah is on another one of her food adventures and this time she dragged me along with her. We're trying to make our own candy."

"Your own candy!" Mae exclaimed gleefully. Sarah had always been an incredible cook, but she rarely was able to convince Julie to get in on a new food exploration. "Fun!"

"I finally got Julie to join me," yelled Sarah from the background. "Now come on Mae, tell us what's happening!"

"Okay, so! Like I texted earlier, my Jeep broke down and I called for a tow. The truck shows up, and I am not kidding you, THE hottest man EVER was driving it. I died! Are you kidding me?! I look like I ran myself over. His name is Jack Wilder, can you even take it?!"

"Jack Wilder! Come on now?! Does he know he's a leading man in your Christmas romance?" Julie laughed.

"Julie!" Mae squealed.

"With a name like that! Jack. Wilder." Sarah took a moment to ponder and then went back to doing what looked like rolling the candy mix.

"Sarah!" Mae squealed again. "So, he gives us a tow and it turns out he's a Forest Ranger."

"Are you making this up?" Sarah stopped whatever she was doing and walked over closer to the phone.

"No," responded Mae earnestly. "It gets crazier! We get back to the garage. We're in this cute little mountain town that looks like a for real Christmas story and THEN I find out Jack has a dog named after Samwise Gamgee. STOP IT. I almost died, again."

"Did you drop a few quotes on him?" Julie asked.

"I figured I'd wait to hit him with the good stuff. I didn't want to give it all up at once, you know." Mae pretended that was the real reason she hadn't said anything and not because her throat had closed over.

"Smart," Julie laughed again. "You wouldn't want him to lose himself too quickly."

"At least not until I've showered," Mae said giving herself a once over in the mirror. She looked like a woman who had been driving for years, decades even.

"Rex, the man who owns the garage, ordered the part for my Jeep. He said I should be ready in two days or so."

"That's not too bad!" Said always positive Sarah.

"Seems like a nice place to write."

"Or to do some other things that might have inspirational value," Julie added mischievously.

"Julie!" Mae pretended that she was appalled. "Speaking of writing, I didn't get to tell you the other crazy thing. The woman who owns this place, Mitzey, she's a fan of my books. She has them here, in the motel. She called me a real author!"

"MAE! You are a real author," Julie chastised. "You have got to get out of this self-sabotaging headspace you're in. It's no good!"

"Ugh. I guess I'm still struggling with that Elizabeth Birk conversation. And writer's block. Sorry to sound…needy?" Mae shook her head as if trying to get the insecure thoughts out.

"Well, I am very glad you met a new fan of your books Mae," Sarah said as she dipped her finger into whatever good stuff was now in the mixing bowl.

"Yeah, and tell us some more about that handsome Jack with his *Lord of the Ring* references and big tow truck." Julie teased.

"JULIE!" Mae yelled again. "He is very handsome. But he lives here, and I live… I guess I live in New Hampshire now, don't I?" There was a long pause as Mae processed that she no longer lived in LA.

"Well, I hear they have a lot of forests in New Hampshire, so you never know what's gonna happen!" Julie the director was determined to turn Mae's life into a movie.

"This is not a Christmas romance story!" Mae said again adamantly.

"We're so glad you called and that you and Scarpetta are okay." Sarah blew kisses at Mae.

"Thank you. I miss you both already!" Mae waved into the phone at her friends.

"Miss you too," said Julie. "Now get some sleep so you can go to a Christmas tree farm or a cookie bakeoff or something along those lines with handsome Jack. Keep us posted!"

"Julie!" Mae giggled one more time before waving again and hanging up. Scarpetta was already laying on the bed like she owned the place and Mae did a dramatic fall down next to her. "A Christmas tree farm? Come on!"

Chapter 7 - Pancakes and Panic Attacks

*M*ae was seated in the sunny dining area of Mitzey's Motel. A few other patrons were scattered around tables enjoying their breakfast. Like all of the rooms Mae had visited in Mitzey's, the space was done up in full holiday regalia. Mitzey was busy bustling around the room, making sure everyone had what they needed. Mae was situated at a table by the window, which was also close to an outlet so she could work on her laptop. She was staring at her screen when Mitzey came by.

"How are the pancakes?" Mitzey posed this as a question but was already beaming with pride as she clearly knew what she had going.

"Oh Mitzey, they are extraordinary!" Mae confirmed. The pancakes were so good that Mae had already devoured them entirely and was secretly thinking she should drag her finger across the plate to catch any bits she might have missed. Unfortunately, Mitzey picked up the plate before Mae had the opportunity to throw herself across that dining etiquette breach.

"Oh, thank you! They were my dad's special recipe." Mitzey's smile was wide but Mae caught a passing melancholy look in her eyes. "Would you like more coffee?"

"Yes, please, that would be wonderful. I really appreciate it." Never enough coffee was Mae's motto.

"I see you're over here typing away," Mitzey said excitedly. "Working on the next Laela? Oh my, where are my manners? I don't mean to pry... It just feels like I'm getting the super inside scoop!"

"I wish I was typing away! To be totally candid, I'm having a bit of writer's block," confided Mae. At that moment, the sound of a door banging on its hinges caught the two women's attention and they turned to look out the window where they could see Jack opening the garage across the street.

"Maybe you will find the perfect muse right here in Warbler Cross." Mitzey winked at Mae who had already started to blush. "I'll be right back with your coffee." She hustled off before Mae could say anything in her defense.

When breakfast was finished, Mae headed across the street to check on the status of her vehicle. She was subtly hoping that maybe now that she'd had some sleep, Jack's presence wouldn't do such a number on her senses. Or, maybe Jack had become very unattractive overnight and developed into the kind of person who cut women off when they were talking, or, who didn't love dogs and *Lord of the Rings* and she could stop thinking he was so perfect. Anything that would deter Mae's entire being from lighting up every time the man smiled. Mae decided that it definitely was possible that her hormones were off from all the traveling. And now that they'd had time to recalibrate, perhaps she wouldn't fall all over herself. Rex was in the back office talking to Jack as Mae walked in with Scarpetta trailing close behind. Upon hearing someone enter, the two men turned towards Mae and Jack broke into a wide smile. Mae's blood immediately started to buzz. No such luck, she thought.

"Good morning, Mae and Scarpetta!" Jack waved. Scarpetta danced over to give Sammy a friendly smell. The pup seemed to mildly tolerate Scarpetta's presence.

"Almost feels like progress," said Mae, recognizing she was much safer when her attention was on the dogs rather than on the man.

"I hope you slept well your first night here in Warbler Cross," Jack said. Mae mentally added *gracious host* to her gaga list.

"Oh, I did, thank you. Mitzey is SUCH a gem. And those pancakes, wow! You weren't kidding Rex!" Mae was already excited for tomorrow's breakfast.

"Nobody can make you feel at home like Mitzey. She's a real talent! A genuine heart of gold that one." Rex said this with such passion that even the dogs stopped to eyeball him.

"A real talent," repeated Mae. "Hmmmmmm. How long have you two been across the street from each other Rex?"

"Oh, about as long as I can remember," Rex said. Mae thought she could detect a hint of pink coming up his neck. Seeming to want to evade further scrutiny he grabbed another rag and walked over to Mae's vehicle, deftly closing the subject. Jack shrugged with a smile and followed him over. Well, that was *very* interesting indeed, Mae thought. Obviously, there was a little something-something between the two neighbors and she was hot to uncover it. As Mae started to follow, she caught a glimpse of a photo on the wall. It was Jack in his Forest Service uniform somewhere out in the mountain woods. Jack's smile was radiating, clearly in his element. He looked so happy. He also, Mae noted, looked pretty good in the pants, too.

"I ordered your part." Rex's voice cut into Mae's thoughts before she could further contemplate any other of the uniform's benefits. "I was able to guarantee delivery for early tomorrow. It won't take too long to swap out. I can have you back on the road by ten thirty tomorrow morning at the latest."

"Oh, my goodness, Rex that is wonderful news. I really appreciate it!" Mae was both relieved and a little bummed that she wouldn't be forced to spend any more time with the fine citizens of the town

"We have a local Christmas Fair this evening," Rex continued. "There's a community supper and even a cookie walk. It's definitely worth checking out. It's just down the street at the Warbler Cross Town Hall."

"Thank you, Rex," Mae nodded her head. OF COURSE, there's a holiday fair she thought. She really was staying in Christmasland. Mae laughed to herself. "I'm just going to step out and text my mom the news. Really grateful for all your help."

Mae exited the front and had just finished messaging her mom with an update about the Jeep when Jack came out to join her in the crisp bright morning air.

"It's a gorgeous day," Jack said as he looked up towards the mountains. "If you and Scarpetta want to

The Holiday Breakdown

stretch your legs, I could take you on one of my favorite walks in the area. Maybe this afternoon? I would have you back in time for the Christmas Fair."

"I feel like I should get more work done," Mae said. She reminded herself that she really did have to get some writing done, but then again, when did a girl get to spend a full twenty-four hours inside a holiday town? "But...who could pass up a private trail tour?"

"Great! Why don't I swing by Mitzey's around oneish? I'll to take you two to a little lookout by a lake. We won't be going up high, so we don't have to worry about gear. Just a nice loop trail," Jack explained enthusiastically.

"Sounds perfect. Thanks!" Mae was very excited but didn't want to fawn all over herself. "See you then." She turned and headed across the street to the motel, stealing a quick glance back at Jack before she stepped inside. "Boy I'd like to deck those halls," she whispered down to Scarpetta. Then she immediately rolled her eyes after hearing the words come out of her own mouth. She couldn't believe she'd said that out loud. Scarpetta flashed her back a look which suggested that she couldn't believe Mae had said that either. *Deck those halls?* So embarrassing, Mae thought as she did one more eye roll for good measure. As Mae walked through the lobby her phone started to vibrate with incoming texts. It was her mother:

A slight problem came up. Hate to burden you when you're dealing with car stuff. Did you have a good breakfast?

"Oh no, what now?!" Mae panicked and immediately looked to Scarpetta for answers. "Did you notice Mom likes to drop an anxiety bomb and then talk about meals? 'I heard aliens were invading. Did you have a good lunch?' Ugh!" She put in her earbuds for the call home. Upon hearing her mom pick up Mae immediately cut in and skipped any salutations, "Mom what's up? Are you and dad alright?"

"Your father and I are fine. I didn't mean to startle you. I wanted to tell you because we just found out that Brian, you know Brian honey, he takes care of our trails and…"

Mae jumped in to speed the information train along, "Yes, I know Brian mom."

"OK, well, Brian was offered a last-minute job in Montana. Apparently, he has a cousin there. It's like a groundskeeper job and he…"

"When is he leaving?" Mae jumped in again.

"They would need him immediately so he's leaving tomorrow. It has benefits honey, full health insurance, including dental! He felt so bad, but of course he should take it. We only have part-time work." Gloria Robards wanted to make sure that everyone in the world had a good dental plan and Mae really did love that quality about her. Her mom continued, "We watched that movie last night about the woman who was orphaned and then posed as a young man to work in a steel factory. Thank goodness she ends up reuniting with her mom who, in fact, always wanted to keep her and…"

Mae cut in again. "I hadn't watched it yet but good to know how it ends. Okay I gotta go."

"We don't want you to feel like you have to do any work at the ski center until after you finish your book, Mae. That's really important to us," Gloria said strongly.

"I appreciate that mom. Really. We'll figure it out! And thanks for letting me know. I'll check in later."

"Bye, honey. Have a good lunch!" Gloria managed to squeeze in one more meal reference before hanging up.

Mae crouched down and gave Scarpetta a head scratch. The pooch, obviously sensing Mae's exasperation, rested her head on Mae's arm. It was

Mae's favorite it's-gonna-be-ok move and she found it to be extremely comforting.

Less than a half an hour later, Mae was back at her computer again. She had chosen to sit near the beautifully decorated Christmas tree in Mitzey's lobby area to write. Mae was hopeful that the twinkling lights and smell of the tree would ignite some magic. Scarpetta lay nearby looking hopeful that someone might drop some food. Mae was staring at her screen when Mitzey came over with a tray of coffee.

"It's just so exciting! You know what's going to happen to Laela before anyone else in the entire world does. And, it's all happening right here, in my motel!" Mitzey beamed as she put down the tray for Mae.

"Well, it seems like maybe even I don't know what's happening." Mae tried to joke as she poured herself a cup. Delighted by the aroma, Mae took a sip of the steaming beverage. She usually didn't tell people about her writing process, but something about Mitzey with her delicious coffee and her love of thriller novels, made Mae want to open up and share.

"I know you'll figure it out," Mitzey responded resolutely. Her expression then slowly shifted into a mischievous smile. "I bet that hike with Jack will help to clear your head."

"What?" Mae blushed again. "I mean a little exercise always does do wonders for the brain." Scarpetta raised her head at this comment, and even to Mae's own ears she sounded full of it.

"Yeah, uh-huh. That's what I meant." Mitzey winked. "We have beautiful trails around here and there is no better guide than Jack. It's really a shame about those budget cuts."

"Is he losing his job?" Mae asked, shocked.

"Oh my… I'm sorry I didn't realize he hadn't…" Mitzey stammered. "Well, I probably shouldn't be saying anything, but due to financial reasons the Forest Service had to let go of someone from this area and before they made their final decision Jack told them to give the job to his partner, Justin. Justin is a single dad and Jack just felt like he needed it more. Jack is hoping they can place him somewhere else or that the job will come back in the summer."

"Oh," Mae thought back to the photo she saw of Jack in Rex's office. He looked so happy in his Forest Service uniform out in the woods. "That sounds really hard.

And, so incredibly kind of him to care about his partner like that."

"Yeah… Jack is like that, a very big-hearted person," Mitzey responded thoughtfully.

"You would think he would have a girlfriend." The words just slipped out before Mae could stop them. It felt like it was none of her business but also how could this amazing masterpiece not be off the market.

"Jack is a wonderful man," Mitzey said, as she gave Mae a look that suggested she was about to give her the full scoop. Mae took another sip of coffee to properly prepare herself. "He is a wonderful man who really loves the woods. He will be out there for days and days, weeks even. One time he left to help with an emergency in a park in Alaska and was gone for months. He hasn't found someone who gets that, yet."

"Oh…" Mae pondered. Then realizing that Mitzey was reading her a little too well, she abruptly switched topics. "What's happening with you and Rex?"

"Rex?!" Mitzey immediately became flustered. "What? Nothing! We're just old friends." As if suddenly bewildered, she stood up, fumbled with her apron and then grabbed the tray. "I need to head back to the kitchen."

81

"Well, how about that?" Mae raised a questioning eyebrow to Scarpetta.

Chapter 8 - He Got Puns

Mae, Jack, Scarpetta, and Sammy had stopped along the trail at a lookout by a beautiful lake. Jack had chosen a rolling loop that meandered through the woods and had a gorgeous view of the mountains above them. He pulled a thermos out of his pack along with a tin dish which he placed on the ground near Sammy. Upon seeing Jack pour the water, Scarpetta danced over to check it out and Jack tapped the bowl to invite Scarpetta to take a sip as well. Sammy took a few steps back, looking up a Jack with a *what is this nonsense* kind of expression on his cute scruffy face.

"Get in there Sammy, she's not gonna hurt ya!" Jack cheered. Scarpetta, who must have sensed the situation, stepped back a tad to make room. After a brief pause, Sammy very hesitantly scooted in to test the water.

"Well, check that out. Wonders never cease!" Mae smiled at the dogs and what seemed to be the huge progress made. She took a water bottle out of her own bag and turned to take in the spectacular view.

"Amazing," she said as she looked out at stunning scene.

"Beautiful," Jack breathed deeply in agreement, which caused Mae to spill a little water down her chin.

She tried to wipe it away (very casually), as they stood there in silence listening to the trees bend and the water ripple in the light wind.

"It's none of my business, but... I guess, when has that ever stopped me?" Mae tried to laugh but it came out more like a gulp. "I heard you gave your job to your forestry partner. I mean, I don't know if that's the right term but..." She trailed off, feeling slightly bad that she was prying, but also at the same time absolutely wanting to pry.

"Oh, you heard, huh?" Jack said without a hint of malice. "I assume it was Mitzey, always trying to make me look good." Mae thought that it didn't take much to make this man look good. Jack continued, "I mentioned to you in the truck that this was a down time for work... I guess the whole story just felt like a lot to tell a person up top."

"Of course. You're totally right, and, obviously not my business at all. I guess I've always just been a too-much-up-top kind of a person." Mae laugh gulped again. *A too-much-up-top kind of person?!* Such a ridiculous thing to say, she chided herself.

"There was only enough in the budget for one full-time person from this area for the season. Justin is a single dad with a mortgage, he needs it more than me." Jack explained.

"So, Rex is keeping you on until your job comes back in the summer? Sorry, there I go again…" Mae continued to pry away, hating herself for it, but committed to getting the story. She was a woman divided: her brain versus her…other parts.

"No, it's totally fine. There are more stations in the surrounding areas that I've put in for. Also, I'm hoping that other full-time positions will open up at different parks in the near future. I can kick around here until the summer, if need be, but I know Rex doesn't really need my help. He's just throwing us a bone." On the word *bone* Jack winked at Sammy. Brutal, Mae thought in response to his pun, and shook her head. But also, she pondered, never had a pun seemed so flippin' cute! Upon this realization, Mae decided that she was going to throw up on herself as soon as she got back to the motel.

"What about you Ms. Mae?" Jack asked.

"What about me what part?"

"What about you—author, driver, formally of LA, headed to New Hampshire-er?" Jack sat down on a nearby tree stump ready to hear the goods.

"Oh, that... You know... I don't know!" Mae laughed, suddenly feeling very self-conscious. It was so much better when she was asking the questions. "Um... I was raised in Snow Creek, New Hampshire. It's near the White Mountains, so just up these Appalachians a ways. It's really beautiful. You'd love it, I think." Ugh! Why did she have to add that Jack would like it? Mae kicked herself mentally. "My parents run a small cross country ski center. When I was growing up all I wanted to do was get out. And I did. I went to college in New York City for creative writing. I've always just been a real book nerd, I guess. Anyways, took me a while but I ended up finishing my first book, which was actually a collection of short stories, one of which ended up leading to my Laela series. After that, I hooked up with a literary agent who was in LA and even though it was really not a problem for me to stay in New York, I knew it was time for a change. I deeply love that city, but I was tired of my bed touching three out of the four walls in my apartment." Mae laughed at the memory. "So, I packed up and moved to Los Angeles. Sorry, I'm talking so much..."

"No, go on," Jack said intently.

"Well, long story still very long. I was out walking Scarpetta at the beginning of this year and I saw a man get out of his car with a bunch of groceries. He rang a doorbell, put the bags down and stepped away. A woman came outside but she didn't leave the steps. They so clearly wanted to hug each other and I could only assume from the scene that they were family. I think she must have been sick or something and they were trying to see each while still keeping her safe. It was sad. And beautiful. I immediately thought, I need to be closer to home. And that's when it hit me, that after all these years, I still thought of Snow Creek as my home. I guess I spent the year trying to ignore it but then my parents called and said that they were going to have to sell the ski center because they couldn't keep it up anymore. And, I just knew I had to go, that it was time for another big change." Mae took a deep breath. She couldn't believe she had shared all that.

"It does seem like you have the perfect career to be able to work from anywhere." Jack's words echoed Mae's hopes.

"Yeah, I just keep telling myself that I'm shifting gears but it will all work out." Mae repeated the sentence that she'd been saying over and over again in her head since the day she'd first made the decision.

"Well," smiled Jack. "It is Christmas after all."

"It is indeed." Mae responded as she wondered who was this man? He's too perfect. *Lord of the Rings* AND Christmas references. She couldn't take it.

"Snow Creek, huh? I actually worked with a guy from up there. We both were in Alaska trying to help out with an emergency in one of the parks. Derek Mumfen? Derek muhhhhhhhh..." Jack was searching his memory for the last name.

"Derek Mumford?" Mae asked.

"Yes! Derek Mumford! I always get his last name wrong because I want to say Derek Muffins."

"Who doesn't?!" Mae giggled enthusiastically and then immediately hated herself for it. She was planning to smack herself as soon as she got a moment alone. She couldn't believe she was acting like such a teenager, babbling on about her life and now cheering for muffins?! What was going on?! Just because the man had the cutest eye crinkles when he smiled and knew his way around a Hobbit reference didn't mean she should act like a silly wildling! She had serious work to do, she reminded herself.

"He's a great guy. Really talked up those New Hampshire mountains, I'll tell ya!" Jack said as he looked around at the dogs who were now sniffing some low branches on a nearby tree. He bent down to grab the now empty water bowl. "OK kids! Pack up your TRUNKS, we better be LEAFING." Jack leaned in on the emphasis of the words to highlight his glaring puns.

"Oh NO!" Mae let out. "Oh no, you did not." Mae paused and then decided that she'd toss one of her own out there. "I'm gonna have to cedar you later. Cedar, see you? It's close? Kinda."

"Looks like someone's been sprucing up their pun work." Jack did it again.

"Well, try not to pine away about it." Mae responded in kind as she packed her water bottle back in her bag. Both dogs stood by, Mae thought they looked embarrassed.

It was late afternoon when Jack pulled up in front of Rex's Garage. Mae hopped out of the pickup and Scarpetta scrambled down behind her.

"Thank you so much for a wonderful time, Jack. We both were so happy to get out and stretch our legs," Mae said as she grabbed her bag from the back.

"Us too! So glad you could come out," Jack said and stepped out of the truck. "I have some errands to run but how would you feel about maybe checking out the Christmas Fair and Community Dinner later?" He paused hesitantly and then added, "I'm sure you have writing to do but as your tow man I feel responsible for you until your vehicle is ready."

"Oh! Oh, well, that's very nice of you but..." Mae had not been ready to be invited to a Christmas Fair.

"I realize now that the term *tow man* may have been slightly off-putting," Jack said easily and then looked down at Sammy with a laugh. "Yeesh! What can I tell ya? I am outta practice buddy."

Mae didn't know what he was out of practice for and assumed that he was just trying to be polite with his continued use of ridiculously humorous word choices and kind invitations. Mae was practically tripping over herself to spend time with this guy, but also felt like she really should just stay inside and write. Then again, when did a person get such an opportunity as to be invited to a real holiday fete with the hottest *tow man* ever? Even if he was only being polite. In that moment, Mae decided that it was fate (or her lack of upkeep on a very old Jeep) that she'd arrived in this magical LaLa

Christmas dreamland and that it would be downright rude to the Universe to not partake in it.

"You know what, I'd love that. Sure, let's do it. I mean…" Mae stammered. "Let's go! Thank you."

"OK? OK! Great, so I'll come by around six?" Jack asked.

"Six it is." Mae paused. "Oh, actually, how about I meet you there at six? The Warbler Cross Town Hall is just down the street, yeah?"

"No problem! Yes, right across the square." Jack pointed. "I'll wait out front."

"OK, perfect. See you then!" Mae smiled and turned to walk towards Mitzey's before she visibly started sweating in front of Jack. A Christmas Fair!

After Mae had crossed the street, she turned just in time to catch a glimpse of Jack before the door to Rex's closed behind him. Taking a second too long to stare after him, Mae tripped and fell on the steps. Mortified she tried to pretend like it was a cool and intentional move. Immediately she began searching for something on the ground. Perhaps she had lost an imaginary silver dollar! That was a totally plausible thing that could have happened, Mae told herself. Scarpetta looked over at her with what seemed to be an incredulous expression. Clearly, she was not one bit fooled.

Chapter 9 - Christmas Fairs Do Make a Girl Feel Impulsive

Mae was running around the room in her bathrobe throwing clothes everywhere. It really didn't matter how many bags Mae rummaged through she just didn't seem to have anything that was Christmas Fair appropriate. She had never really considered herself to be a particularly stylish person, and always ended up referring to her friends when it came to picking outfits. Now, here she was, out in the wilds, with no holiday ensemble and no nearby friends to tell her to stop wearing all black. Her mom called her mid clothes explosion and Mae positioned the phone on the bureau so she could FaceTime while still continuing to stalk the room in the hopes that she might come across something surprising to wear.

"Mae! It looks like a tornado hit your room! You've only been there one night." Her mom always seemed shocked by Mae's messes, but what would have been genuinely shocking would be if the room had remained organized after Mae had entered it.

"Ma!" Mae walked back to the phone to look at her mom who only had the bottom half of her face in the frame. "I'm going to a Christmas Fair and I can't find anything to wear. At this point I don't even know what I packed, what I shipped, and what I got rid of."

"Wear some color honey!" Her mom advised.

"Mom!" Mae sounded like a teenager even to herself.

"You know those ladies in the Christmas movies always wear red." Her mom added not so subtly.

"Mom, you sound just like Julie," Mae responded. Everyone was trying to turn this trip into a holiday romance story. It was ridiculous. So, what, she was moving home to help save the family business, just happened to breakdown along the way, and met a nice handsome man who'd invited her to a holiday fair? That was totally normal. It could happen to anyone! And, furthermore, no matter how Christmas the circumstances appeared to be, it still didn't mean that Mae actually owned any red clothing. She decided to opt for her favorite black onesie and dress it up with her white Doc Martens. White boots were sort of holidayish? She pulled out the wipes she kept for Scarpetta's paws to try and clean the soles, hoping she could maintain looking crisp for one night.

"Your dad is home!" Mae's mom's voice interrupted her thoughts.

"Hey Mae, honey! How's it going with the Jeep?" Kurt Robards stuck his ear into view.

"The part is arriving first thing in the morning," Mae responded. "I just confirmed with Rex, Rex of Rex's Garage. He said he would open early and have me out by late morning. I figure I'll make tomorrow a slightly shorter driving day and stop in Pennsylvania for the night. Then Thursday evening I'll be home!"

"We are very excited to have you here." Mae's dad seemed genuinely happy about it which made Mae feel good.

"Tell him about Jack, honey!" Gloria Robards prodded.

"Mom!" Teenage Mae was back.

"What?!" Gloria Robards, acting coy.

"I feel like you're hinting at something that isn't happening," Mae griped. "Dad, Jack is the local Forest Ranger here, but he just got laid off due to cutbacks..."

"Isn't that just horrible!" Mae's mom was always deeply in tune with the feelings of any given situation—a compassionate trait that Mae very much admired.

"Dad, I was actually hoping that you'd ask Derek Mumford what he thought about Jack. Apparently, they worked together on a job in Alaska. Could you reach out to him tonight, please, and get back to me? I'd appreciate it." Mae was hatching an impulsive and ludicrous plan.

"Yeah, sure honey!" Kurt Robards responded as the entire right side of his face made it on to the screen.

"Mae says they only had one position and Jack gave it to the other Ranger because he has a kid. Sounds like a *very* nice man!" Mae's mom filling in the important emotional details.

"He's working at the garage currently and… anyways, he took us for a quick hike today and invited me to the Christmas Fair tonight." Mae might have blushed but she decided it must just be because of the steam left over in the room from the hot shower.

"Also, the woman whose motel she's staying at likes Mae's books. So that's nice!" Gloria said, continuing to paint the full sentimental landscape.

"Yes, that was really nice. Everyone here is lovely," Mae took a beat. "I might have some ideas about Brian's job."

"These ideas wouldn't have to do with a handsome, recently out of work, Forest Ranger, would they?" Her mom teased.

"MOMMMMMMMMMMM! I never said he was handsome!" Mae weakly contested.

"Then why are you having so much trouble picking an outfit?" Mae's dad posited with a zinger.

"DAD! Not you too! Just ask Derek and text me back, OK? Please?" Mae knew they were on to her.

"You got it honey," her dad winked.

"Do you know if this handsome Jack likes soup?" Her mom asked as if that was a totally normal follow-up question.

"Soup? Mom, I don't know! What a random thing to ask! I mean, who doesn't like soup?"

"You don't," Gloria Robards responded matter-of-factly.

"I don't not like soup as a rule, mom. You just practically drowned me in it growing up. I was overwhelmed by soup. I'm still recuperating. Anyways! I gotta go." Mae needed to finish getting dressed so she could get to the Christmas Fair on time. She felt slightly ridiculous thinking about it now. What was going to happen next? She wondered if perhaps she'd suddenly be asked to judge a cookie bakeoff?

"Night, honey!" Both of Mae's parents said, at the same time, interrupting Mae's Hallmark Christmas movie flight of fancy. Their phone was now facing the ceiling so she couldn't see either of them, but she waved regardless before clicking off the call.

Prior to heading out for the evening's festivities, Mae walked and fed Scarpetta. "Wish me luck," she said to her pooch before dropping a kiss on that beautifully perfect wet nose and slipping out the door. Mae had wanted to meet Jack out in front of the Town Hall so she would have the cool walk over to clear her head. She had so much on her mind. Mae pushed away the feelings of guilt that she was not, at that very moment, sitting at her computer writing. When did a girl have an opportunity like this?! It was only one night and of course she would get the book done, she promised herself. As she crossed the square, she admired the beautiful decorations and twinkling lights on all the trees. The people of Warbler Cross had certainly done the most amazing job dressing the town up in holiday spirit. Music drifted towards her, coming from the large building up ahead at the end of the path. There were people strolling in and out of the brightly lit entryway. Off to the left Mae could see the silhouette of a man leaning against one of the building's pillars and by the immediate temperature rise inside her jacket, she knew it was Jack. Mae waved and walked over.

"What a fine evening!" Jack smiled.

"It is gorgeous. Such great decorations! Wow, you guys really do it up." Mae was throwing all the enthusiasm she was feeling deep in her cockles for Jack into her words about the event. She assured herself that she sounded totally normal as she stuffed her hands inside her jacket pockets so she wouldn't fidget.

"Shall we?" Jack opened the door for Mae.

"Thanks," Mae said. She smiled as they entered and took in the holiday scene. The Warbler Cross Town Hall dazzled in full green and red regalia. Evergreen garlands hung along the walls with big bright bows and pinecones covered in glitter tied at every corner. A huge Christmas tree took its place in the center of the room with sparkling ornaments and white lights that danced throughout the branches. There was a buffet line and tables stacked with Christmas Fair items for purchase. Crocheted seasonal potholders, wreaths, handmade scarves, and the famous cookie walk lined the sides of the large room. Mae genuinely loved a good cookie walk and was thrilled to see people queued up to pick out a beautifully decorated tin so they could fill it with as many goodies as would fit. Round tables with chairs took up the middle area surrounding the tree where people had gathered to eat and commune. Mae wanted to take a picture to send to Julie, it was all so cute and perfect.

"Nice to see you both again so soon!" Mae turned to see Mitzey sitting at the welcome table. She winked at Mae whose face immediately flushed.

"Oh, there's Rex," Mae responded in kind, pointing just past Mitzey to where Rex could be seen talking with a group of people. "Did you see him too?" Mae gave Mitzey a little gotcha-type smile.

"Tickets for the buffet?" Mitzey grimaced. Jack and Mae each purchased an admission to the community dinner which turned out to also be a fundraiser for the local food pantry.

"Let's hit it!" Jack said, enthusiastically grabbing the red paper plate that served both as their ticket and their vehicle for eating. The three nodded to each other as Mae and Jack set off down the line picking which holiday dishes to treat themselves to. Everyone at the buffet was saying hello to Jack and wishing him a Happy Holiday. He was clearly very dear to all the people of Warbler Cross, Mae thought. After piling everything that could fit onto their plates, the two made their way across the room to the table where Rex was sitting.

"Hey Rex! May we join you?" Mae asked smiling. Everything smelled so good, she couldn't wait to taste all the goods she had chosen.

"Please!" Rex said as he moved a cup full of silverware out of the way so Mae could put her plate down.

"Hey," said Jack as he put down his food and waved at someone over by the cookie tables. "Would you both excuse me for a second, please? I want to say a quick hello to Justin over there. Don't wait for me to start."

"Justin is his friend from the Forest Service," Rex explained to Mae as Jack crossed the room.

"I heard," Mae responded earnestly. And then, perhaps prying again, "It must be good to have him helping out."

"I love having Jack around. We all love having Jack around! But I don't really have enough work to keep him for long I'm afraid. Jack knows this. It's just temporary until he finds another placement."

Mae nodded sympathetically, and then they both sat in silence, focused on working their way through their respective plates. After a particularly delicious bite of

101

some kind of doctored up stuffing Mae asked, "How long have you and Mitzey been friends?"

Rex's face very subtly changed color. "We've been friends since she moved here from New Mexico to take care of her dad and the motel. She really put her heart and soul into that place and into taking care of him."

"Oh…" Mae responded, now more fully understanding Mitzey's reference to her father. "She really is an incredible person. Have you two ever been, ummm, more than friends?"

"What? No!" Rex protested. "We are supportive, across the street, business owning neighbors. I wouldn't want to be disrespectful."

"Friends AND supportive across the street business owners slash neighbors. Wow, Rex! Of course, you wouldn't want to be disrespectful, but I get the idea that you two are both waiting for the other one to say something. Maybe on Christmas you could bring her over something to go with those pancakes?" Mae hinted not so subtly.

"I don't even know what you are talking about!" Rex's complexion turned a deeper shade.

"Oh, you don't, do ya?" Mae laughed. Just then her phone beeped announcing that a message had arrived.

"Excuse me for a second will you please, Rex?" Mae took out her phone and saw it was a text from her dad:

Talked to Derek. Says Jack is a real upstanding man. They worked together in Alaska for a couple of months. Says Jack is good person.

Mae was delighted by her dad's text. She had assumed it would be a glowing review, but it felt like the smart thing to do was just to double check with the person they knew in common. Her phone beeped again:

For what it's worth Mae, you've always been a great judge of character and I support whatever you think is right. Will be great to have you here.

Mae was very touched by her dad's text. She started writing multiple texts back, trying to express how much she appreciated the good words of faith but kept deleting them because they seemed somehow silly. She finally landed on a simple response:

Thanks Dad. I really really appreciate it. Means a lot to me.

Mae added a heart emoji for good measure and then put her phone away. She ate some more of the glorious stuffing while taking a moment to gather herself. Mae pondered if she about to do something that was quite possibly very rash but was pulled out of her thoughts as she felt someone sit down next to her. She turned to see the upbeat face of a young woman.

"Hi! I'm Koral Farsad!" She introduced herself and smiled at Mae. "I own the bookstore down the street. A little birdie told me that you're THE Mae Robards, author of the *Finding Laela* series. I just wanted to come over and tell you how much I love your books." At this moment Jack returned and stood behind Koral.

"THE Mae Robards." He winked.

"I...thank you," Mae stammered. "Thank you so much! I'm delighted you've enjoyed them!"

"Looking forward to the next one. We'll get it for our local book club. Hard copy! We're very into women supporting women here." Koral got up and gave Mae's arm a kind squooch. If Mae hadn't already been sitting down, she would have been swept off her feet by the kindness. Koral waved at someone across the room and started to leave but turned to Mae with a last-minute thought. "Might I also add that our Jack looks suspiciously like your Detective Williams, but you hadn't met him yet when you started writing the series had you?" And then she was off, leaving Mae in a sea of wide eyed bewilderment.

"I don't even know what she's talking about," Mae said, repeating Rex's words from earlier, and setting her face in a look of fierce denial that any of her characters might have any resemblance to Jack. Then Mae jumped up, as if remembering that she had somewhere to be. It was such a quick movement that she tripped over the leg of her chair and fell into Jack, who caught her, but not before stumbling briefly himself. He looked at Mae, with her intensely serious expression, and suddenly burst into a glorious laughter. It was all so ridiculous, Mae thought as she wiped off some of the holiday dinner that she'd spilled on her pants, and then she too broke out into madcap laughs. She wished she could just stick her head inside the turkey.

The air was still filled with mirth when Mae and Jack exited the Town Hall later that evening to head back across the square to the motel. A stuffed cookie tin and a few charming stitched items that Mae had bought as gifts were tucked safely in her bag. The sounds of merriment floated around them as the two made their way through the gorgeous Christmas trees that lit up the path.

"They've done such a wonderful job decorating," admired Mae again. "Everyone here is just so delightful!"

"Aren't they? This town has been very good to me." Jack's words made Mae smile. She'd liked to be very good to him, she thought. Then she immediately tried to un-smile because she was afraid Jack might be able to read her mind. Get it together woman, she scolded herself, you have decisions to make and there's major work to be done! Jack continued, "They've all been really wonderful."

"Have been?" Mae asked. "Sounds like you're planning on leaving. Would you like to wait and see if your job or a job in this area opens up? Or are you thinking that you'll probably go?" Mae had made the full transition into being all up in Jack's business. No time to be shy now she thought, she was about to do something outrageous.

"I mean, a job might open up here, but if something comes up somewhere else first, I'm going to take it. I don't want to be a burden to Rex. I've started actively looking for other posts." Jack stopped walking and stood for a moment, thoughtfully.

"Something else, huh?" Mae took a big beat. This was the moment. "What if you came with me?"

"Pardon?" Jack asked as if he hadn't heard her correctly.

Mae was immediately so embarrassed of the sentence that had just come out of her mouth. Wishing she could inhale it back into her face and un-ask the question, she started talking extremely fast as if that might cause a rewind. "We need someone to help maintain trails, watch over the woods basically, for the ski center. You obviously seem to love the woods, and while it's not a full-time job, there is room and board. We have a cabin in the back." Jack was staring at her. She felt so dumb. What was she thinking asking someone who was practically a stranger?! She wished she could get in her Jeep and drive away right now. Mae glanced around the square for an escape route as words tumbled faster out of her mouth. "Sorry, it was silly that I asked. I just thought you might need a place for the winter or until another job comes along. And I need someone to help. We, we need someone. Our trails person just left today. TODAY! And I'm on a writing deadline and having a breakdown. I mean my Jeep broke down. And then he leaves, today! Of course, I just met you and you don't know me." Mae paused half a second to take a breath. "I mean we have to hire someone, so chances are we won't know them too well either, so maybe it's not that weird? You could ask Derek! Derek knows us. Anyways! Dumb I said anything. Never mind. It was just a brainstorm. Let's forget it ever came up."

Mae tightened her scarf around her neck and turned to walk-run away, stepping directly into a tree branch. Jack grabbed her arm so she didn't fall from the impact.

Mae's blush blushed. Could she be more humiliated? No, she decided. This was the absolute worst.

"Thank you for asking me," Jack said kindly.

"I was only asking you as a professional courtesy," Mae added very dishonestly. "I don't want you to think I invite every man, who may or may not have some similarities to any of my characters, back to my hometown. You seem like a responsible person. We need help and I thought you might be looking for a place for a few months…"

"I didn't take it any other way," Jack said. "And, I appreciate the professional courtesy." He paused. "So, I do have similarities then? To one of your characters, I mean."

"I guess he has brown hair, or whatever." Mae's heart was suddenly beating so hard that her off brand *YouAreSoFit* watch started beeping thinking she was working out again.

"What's that beeping?" Jack asked looking around.

"It's my watch. It must need to be recharged." Mae pulled her sleeve further down on her wrist and stuck her arm behind her back. Mortified, she felt her entire body turning seven shades of red.

"Hmmmm. OK." There was a very long pause as the two stood staring at each other. Holiday lights twinkled around them in the late evening sky. Their breath was forming cold clouds in the air yet it was somehow very hot inside Mae's jacket.

"OK, what?" Mae asked hesitantly.

"OK I'll take the job," Jack responded.

"Really?" Mae's legs went out a little bit from under her, but she caught herself, hopefully without being too obvious about it.

"Really." Jack replied seriously. "I hope you don't mind I texted Derek after our hike."

"I did too." Mae squinted slightly in admission. "Or, I asked my dad to at least."

"He said great things about you and your family." Jack smiled. The two stood in silence for a moment and Mae didn't know what to say next as a follow-up. "All right so... I guess we'll need to be ready to leave tomorrow morning then?" Jack asked, just getting right down to it. "I assume this starts immediately."

"I mean, that would be perfect. Would you be ready to go that quick? I know it's very sudden."

"I don't have a lot of stuff. I like to be able to travel easily and I've just been renting a room from one of Rex's friends since the job ended." Jack stuck his hands in his pockets.

"I'm sure Sammy is going to love Snow Creek." Mae was trying to find a positive yet neutral tone.

"I am sure he will. Let me escort you back to Mitzey's." The two turned and started walking again. "It's not a lot of stuff, but I still definitely have some packing to do. And, well, I gotta prep for a new adventure."

"A new adventure," Mae repeated the phrase thoughtfully as it was also what Sarah had said to her. "I googled a place in Pennsylvania that's just under halfway since tomorrow will be the shorter driving day as we'll probably be setting out a little later. It's an inn just off the highway that takes dogs. Seems like the perfect place to spend the night. Separately, of course!" Mae got more and more flustered throughout her poor explanation. "I mean in the same place but in a different...it's the perfect stop to break up the trip."

"Sounds good." It almost looked as if Jack was stifling another laugh.

The two crossed the remainder of the square in total quiet, both clearly wrapped up in their own thoughts. Mae could not believe what had just happened. She had initiated it, but still, she couldn't believe it. She'd offered Jack the position and he had taken it. Just like that, everything had changed again. Things were getting wilder and wilder!

As they approached the across the street business establishments of Mitzey and Rex's, Mae caught a glimpse of curtains being shifted in the motel window and in the upstairs apartment over the garage. Looks like someone or someONES had been spying on them, Mae thought as she shook her head. Jack appeared to have seen it too as he was also squinting at the lit-up windows.

"We have to find a way to get those two together," Mae said thoughtfully.

"Good luck with that. It would take a miracle for one of them to have the nerve to make the first move," said Jack.

"Well, I certainly believe in Christmas miracles." As soon as Mae said it, she felt cheesy, but at the same time, she totally meant it. It was a constant struggle between the two opposing halves of herself.

"So do I Mae Robards, so do I," Jack responded in agreement. Christmas miracle magic lingered between them in the crisp December night air. Very uncharacteristically Mae almost went to hug Jack, but feeling the need to hamper down her enthusiasm, she took a step back. It's just a working friendship, she reminded herself.

"OK, well… I should get back. As you said, big day tomorrow." Mae made a move to head for Mitzey's.

"Yes, big day!" Agreed Jack. They both took a step towards their respective establishments.

"Thank you, Jack." Mae turned back for a moment. "This will really be a huge help to us."

"Thank you, Mae," Jack replied earnestly. "Sammy and I needed something to come along."

"OK," Mae smiled and walked up the steps to Mitzey's.

"OK," Jack echoed as he headed into Rex's.

Mae entered the lobby and saw Mitzey acting busy behind the registry desk. There was a fresh plate of cookies laid out on the entry table with a hot cocoa station. The mugs were actually in the shape of snowmen with black top hats to keep the beverage warm. Mitzey really goes all out, Mae thought admiringly.

"Good evening! Back so soon?" Mitzey attempted to act surprised.

"Back so soooooon?" Mae mimicked, her tone overflowing with amusement. "Don't play me Mitzey! I saw you snooping. You and Rex are just like Danny Kaye and Vera-Ellen's characters in *White Christmas*. Remember, they try to set up their friends but then *they* also get together, so…. Hmmmmmm Mitzey."

"Uhhhhhhh," Mitzey stammered and then did a verbal one eighty. "Vera-Ellen! Such a tiny waist! Speaking of, I laid out some fresh cookies and hot cocoa."

"Don't think I don't notice that you're disarming me with goodies," Mae commented on Mitzey's masterful topic change maneuver. "But I'll go along with it as these look incredibly delicious! Thank you. And I absolutely love these cup hats. I've never seen anything like them before. So cute!" Mae grabbed a cookie and a cocoa and headed to the couch by the fire.

"Soooooooo..." Mitzey pried.

"Sooooooooooooooo..." Mae repeated, feigning innocence.

"Come on Mae! Don't leave me hanging like this." Mitzey made a plate up for herself and joined Mae on the couch. "We saw you and Jack talking all night."

"Oh, WE did, did WE," Mae poked again. Mitzey reddened and Mae smiled. "Well, since you asked, it just so happens that I asked Jack...well I guess I offered Jack... I thought that maybe he needed some work for the interim and I need some help. Or, me and my parents need..." Mae just couldn't find the right way to phrase it so she didn't sound totally crazy, even to herself. "I'm moving home to help run my parents ski center and I need help with the trails. And, Jack had mentioned that he might need seasonal work. So, I know it seems impulsive, but I thought it could work out for everyone. Professionally of course."

"Oh, of course! Professionally," Mitzey added delightfully.

"Oh, you are so one to talk!" Mae's face reddened again and she took another sip of cocoa to try and swallow the blushing embarrassment she felt. This was all so unlike her! She felt like a silly cliché. But she had to admit to herself, it was very exciting.

Both women drank their cocoa and ate their cookies while Christmas carols played over the small speaker in the corner. Mae looked around shaking her head; she still couldn't believe what she'd just done. Maybe she was in a Christmas story? She smiled at the ridiculous idea and laughed to herself. Whatever was happening, it was a beautiful moment. Unfortunately, Mae's thoughts were abruptly scattered by the vibration of her phone. She groaned as she pulled it out to look. It was Neal:

Avail to talk now?

"Sorry to ruin a perfect scene," Mae sighed. "But I gotta take this." She smiled at Mitzey, thanked her again for the amazing treats and apprehensively headed to her room.

Mae assumed it wasn't great news that Neal needed to relay otherwise he would have just texted it. She decided she would rather hear a bad update while walking, so she grabbed Scarpetta's leash and her earbuds and then headed back out. Scarpetta needed an evening walk anyway and Mae could do with some more mind clearing air. When the two were a block or so away from the motel, Mae made the call. Neal picked up immediately.

"Neal! Hey! What's up?" Mae tried to sound super casual.

"How's it going, Mae? Got your message about the Jeep part. Glad you're all OK. How's the book?"

"I'm writing! I'm writing!" Mae was a little exasperated at Neal's question but also felt totally guilty that she had spent practically the entire day not writing at all.

"You can see why I'd be a little nervous," Neal responded to Mae's tone. "With a third extension, you stuck in Kentucky and now you're just over a week out on your deadline! Sorry, I know you have a lot of life stuff happening at once." He paused briefly. "I spoke with Elizabeth Birk."

"Oh no, OK..." Mae totally stopped walking, stood still for a second, and then started walking again at a much faster gait than before, as if she could somehow outpace any uncomfortable and potentially disagreeable comments. Scarpetta kept up, seemingly recognizing the anxiety shift.

"You know she's very…well, you met her. In a way it's a real compliment Mae; she sees in you the skills of a classical detective author. But she thinks your character tends to go off on disordered, her word, disordered tangents and that you lighten your writing with, ummmm…."

"With what?" Mae prodded.

"With *unnecessary whimsey*, her words."

"Wow. Unnecessary whimsey. OK. So… I'm silly. She thinks my main character's train of thoughts are silly? And, that I enjoy a messy tangent. Which, fine, I'm not going to disagree with that at all as it's absolutely true, but that's the character!" It was the second time that night Mae had felt hot outside in the cold night air, but this time it was for an entirely different reason.

"Mae, I reminded her of your award and of your popularity with your readers," Neal said trying to smooth the situation.

"AND?!" Mae would not be smoothed.

"And she gave me the *Be Better* quote again." Neal sighed.

"Really quite the judgement, don't you think? That something that makes people happy isn't somehow as valuable because it's not strictly serious? That I am somehow lacking because I don't conform to a more austere form of writing. For whatever that means anyway!" Mae was getting worked up. She tried to lower her voice a little as she passed people on the sidewalk.

"Look Mae, it's up to you, obviously. We can leave the publisher if she wants you to change something you feel is integral to your work. This is what we brought to them. As far as I see it, she's changing the terms of the agreement. But I know you need the money right now for the ski center," Neal paused. "It's your writing Mae and I am here to negotiate for you. So, think on it."

"I'll think on it." She took a deep breath, not at all delighted to have even more to think on. "Thanks Neal," Mae added knowing that he did really have her back.

"But think on it while you're writing OK, Mae?!" Neal said, back in pep talk mode. "No matter what you decide about the tone, it's still due. And we need to hold up our end. Alright, I gotta go. We're making a Santa hat for the cat. Bye, Mae!"

"Bye, Neal!" Mae hung up. She breathed deeply and turned back towards the motel. "Would you like a Santa hat?" she asked Scarpetta. "I've always loved a little whimsey. Who wouldn't want some extra?" Scarpetta looked back at her in a manner which suggested that she too was up for some whimsey. Especially if said whimsey involved more doggie treats.

The Holiday Breakdown

Chapter 10 - Ho Ho Ho

Mae, Jack, Mitzey, and Rex were standing in front of the garage. The part for the Jeep had come in early, and, as promised, Rex had immediately set to work installing it. Mae had barely slept at all the night before; a parade of thoughts running through her brain—visions of Jack standing amongst the Christmas lights, her book, her family's cross country ski center, her impulsive decisions, and then back to the beginning to run them again. She'd thought a lot about Elizabeth Birk's comments. She knew it was true, of course, that all good characters grew and progressed. But the idea that her Laela would change by becoming more, more…she didn't even know what exactly. More stable? More structured? It seemed antithetical to the character herself.

Mae had eventually given up on the tossing, turning, and overthinking and had gotten up to work on her book. Then at some point during the night, she'd fallen asleep with her computer open on her bed and had awoken when rays of sunshine started to peak out over the trees and through the window. Mae had jumped up, showered and quickly packed, wanting to squeeze in one last Mitzey breakfast before heading out. Mitzey had even set aside special treats for Mae and Jack to take on their trip, which she was now holding as they all stood next to Mae's Jeep.

"Just a little something for the road," Mitzey said as she gave Mae one of the goodie bags and a steaming hot to-go coffee. Mae placed them on the hood of her vehicle and the two embraced each other in a warm hug.

"Thank you so much Mitzey. I really appreciate all your kindness and generosity!" Mae felt as if she had known this woman for so long even though they had met only days ago. "Do you mind if I grab that photo of us?" Mae asked as she pulled out her phone. The two women got in close and took a bunch of smiling pics. "Put your number and email in my contacts and I'll send these to you," Mae said to Mitzey as she handed her the phone. Mitzey saved her info and then returned Mae's cell. The two women hugged again. Mae turned to Rex. "Thank you, Rex! I couldn't be more grateful!" Mae then gave Rex a hug as well. She grabbed her coffee and baked goods off the hood and got into her Jeep in order to give the others space. "Scarpetta," Mae called to her co-pilot, who had been sniffing something of apparent interest with Sammy over on the side the road. Scarpetta bounded over, jumped into the Jeep, and hopped through to the back where she plunked herself down excitedly for the next leg of the trip. She was a traveling gal! Plus, Mae could tell that she smelled baked goods.

Mae watched as Mitzey, Jack, and Rex huddled around each other. It was easy to see the love between the three of them. Jack's truck was packed with what looked like a couple of stackable bins, a big hiking pack, and a few smaller bags. He definitely travelled light, Mae thought. She got comfortable in her seat and stared down at her phone in an effort to give them a moment of privacy. She pondered the abrupt turn of events as she heard them talking outside and hoped she was doing the right thing.

"OK, well," Jack started. "This is all very last minute, and you both know that you two mean so much to…" Mitzey didn't wait for the rest of it. She lunged at Jack and wrapped him in a huge hug. Jack reached over and pulled Rex into the huddle too. Even the normally shy Sammy looked like he wanted in and scurried under their feet.

"You take care of yourself Jack," Mitzey said wiping her eyes. "Please keep us updated regularly!"

"I will, I will!" Jack promised. He turned to Rex. "Thank you, Rex, for everything. We will miss you."

The Holiday Breakdown

"As Mitz says, this will be great!" Rex seemed to then start getting a little emotional so he nodded his head and bent down to pet Sammy. "Y'all keep us posted," he said to the pup, giving him a good scratch. After a moment he stood back up and put his hands in his pockets. "We'll want to hear from you on Christmas, of course."

"And before, please," Mitzey added.

"And before," Rex agreed.

"Of course," Jack promised.

"Well, alright then…" Rex said as Jack opened the door for Sammy and then got into the driver's seat. Mitzey handed Jack the coffee and treats, then clutched his hand for a quick moment.

Mae recognized that this was the signal for them to leave, so she pulled out into the street and then Jack drove out behind her. Everyone waved and for a brief moment Mae felt like she might cry. She reached into the brown bag and pulled out a freshly glazed chocolate donut that looked so deliciously comforting. Scarpetta eyed her from the back, conveying to Mae the strong signal that she could smell Doggie Trees in there and that Mae had better be forthcoming. Not wanting to withhold any holiday goodness, Mae reached into the bag, found one, and flipped it to Scarpetta. Both women deserved a little baked comfort.

Mae had given Jack the address of the roadside hotel in Pennsylvania where she'd made reservations for their night stopover and they had agreed on a driving route. The two were, however, still trying to stay within visual distance of each other and had decided they'd call when one of them needed to stop.

Mae was almost to the bottom of Mitzey's wonderful brewed coffee when her cell started ringing. Mae glanced down to see that it was Julie and clicked the phone on speaker.

"JULIE!" Mae exclaimed to her friend.

"You did what now?!" Julie jumped right in.

"I see you must have gotten my email?" Mae laughed. She had messaged Julie in the middle of the night about all that had unfolded. Knowing her friend was probably keeping text alerts on while Mae was still on the road, she'd chosen to send an email, trying to respect people's sleep schedules but also wanting Julie to have all the juicy details of what had transpired immediately.

"Mae! Sarah and I are dying over here. Just skip the opening and give us the goods," Julie said and Mae could hear her friend's disbelieving smile coming through the phone.

"I know, I know! It's so rash. Jack needed a job and like I said, we needed a person to tend the trails. It just seemed too coincidental not to ask. I mean for real, it's like it was meant to be." Mae paused and briefly considered beating her head on the steering wheel. "Ughhhhh, I can't believe that I, Mae Robards, just used the phrase *meant to be!* So gross. The other possibility, of course, is that this is totally insane and I'm losing it." Mae was hoping that Julie didn't think her emotional wheels had come off.

"Well," started Julie in her most pragmatic voice. "It does seem extremely perfect that you both know this Derek guy, so you have some sort of reference. Not like in these Christmas movies where people just invite total strangers into their homes. At least you got a character endorsement!" Julie's words had a momentary relieving effect on Mae.

"Thank you, Julie. And this isn't a Christmas movie!" Mae repeated for probably the one hundredth time since she'd first received her parent's phone call. Although, if Mae was honest with herself, it did have some glaring similarities and she hoped that she didn't let herself get so taken with the moment that she lost her (more often than not) good sense.

"Keep telling yourself that Mae," Julie teased. "What did your mom say?"

"She asked me if he likes soup."

Julie erupted into laughter. "Of course, she did!"

"I mean, it IS definitely very sudden." Mae switched from jovial back to the panic she'd been trying to keep at bay, which now that she'd left the warmth of the Christmas town, was starting to scream louder in her head. "I'm so far afield at this point I could mess literally everything up—my career, the ski center, my parents' livelihood, and now Jack's livelihood. What am I doing bringing a man home who I barely know?! I haven't finished my book!"

"MAE!" Julie's voice cut in. "You're spiraling! You made choices. Now stick to your gut. One thing at a time! You get home, you get settled, you write. Then you can figure out all the ski stuff. If something comes up, you can fix it then; no need to let it all fall on you at once." Julie was always so good with reminding Mae that looking backward, second-guessing and worrying about the future (all at the same time) never helped anyone. Not that Mae wasn't going to do it, but it was a good reminder regardless.

Mae breathed in deeply. "You're too good to me, Jules. I really appreciate it. Sorry to keep swinging back and forth, and for all the dumping, ugh! You have every right to break up with me."

"It's not dumping! You're my friend! And I'm not going to break up with you, at least not until Sarah and I have gotten free ski lessons," Julie teased. "Also, we're really enjoying the Jack saga. Tell me again what he looks like when he laughs."

"JULIE!" Mae was back to giggling when a call waiting beeped on her phone. "Oh, my goodness, it's Jack calling through!"

"Take the call! Take the call! He's probably going to sing carols to you." Clearly Julie was deeply milking this moment as Mae hadn't had a crush on anyone in so long.

"Julie!" Mae squealed again. "OK, love you."

"Love you! Text me when you get to the hotel." Julie said as she rung off.

"Hey Jack!" Mae switched over to the other call trying to throw on her most cool, calm, and collected voice. "Everything going alright? Calling to change your mind?"

"Ha! No, have you?" Jack responded. Immediately upon hearing his voice, Mae's whole vehicle felt as if the air had been sucked out of it and she almost knocked her head against the window trying to smack the silly out of herself. Scarpetta eyeballed her from the back probably noticing the immediate shift in pheromone levels. Mae gave her a look in return letting her know that she'd better not mention it. Scarpetta laid back down but her expression suggested that she knew what was up.

"No, we're doing alright. Quite good actually." Mae responded in what she hoped was a very casual yet positive tone. Although she suddenly realized that her casual tone for some reason came off slightly like she was speaking with an English accent. Oh well, Mae gave up and shrugged to herself, who didn't love *The Great British Baking Show?!*

"That sounds promising," Jack laughed, seeming not to notice Mae's quick visit to Britain. "I was calling for something a little less imperative...but, I thought it might be fun if we did a top ten Christmas movies list. Like a road game of sorts."

"That sounds fun!" Mae responded, holding back what she really was thinking: *A Christmas movie list? Are you kidding me? WHO MADE YOU? YOU*

PERFECT MAN! But instead, she just said, "Only ten? So hard. There are too many!"

"Well, I guess first and foremost," started Jack as if this was the most serious topic ever. "Do you count *Die Hard* as Christmas movie?"

"Of course, I do!" Mae was very passionate about this subject.

"As one should," Jack agreed.

"It has a Christmas movie theme song," Mae said, prepared to list all the reasons, as this was clearly an argument she had made before.

"Run DMC," added Jack.

"Yes!" Mae looked back at Scarpetta, impressed. "It takes place at Christmastime and there's even a Santa hat."

"I believe Bruce Willis writes on the guy's sweatshirt, *Now I have a machine gun, HO HO HO.* Which is extremely Christmas-y."

Mae laughed deeply, "Yes! VERY holiday spirit! Also, there is a kiss at the end, which is quintessential Christmas movie." Mae immediately reddened inside her Jeep. Oh no, the thought, why did she bring up kissing?! She gave Scarpetta the what-did-I-do eyeball roll. Scarpetta looked back at her as if she was a madwoman.

"Of course, there is *White Christmas!*" Mae rushed to change the topic.

"Of course!" Jack agreed, going along with Mae's movie jump. "The pinnacle one might say."

The two went back and forth as the highway miles rolled by. They both agreed that Vince Vaughn's performances in *Four Christmases* and *Fred Claus* was comedic genius. And that Paul Giamatti took Santa Claus to a whole new level. As did Kurt Russel in *The Christmas Chronicles*. Both Mae and Jack said that the original animated *Grinch* was their favorite even though they agreed that all the versions had their good points. They discussed the older holiday classics as well, and Mae was having so much fun that she barely noticed as the driving time ticked by until her phone beeped again. This time it was her mother.

"Jack, my mom is calling," Mae said, almost sadly, as she hated to leave the conversation. "I had better take it."

"Of course," Jack replied. "We'll finish the list later."

"Looking forward to it," Mae responded. And she was, very much so. Maybe even a little too much, she thought as she clicked over. "Ma! What's up?"

"It was my shift at the Church Food Pantry this morning, so I missed your call, but your dad said that you offered Jack the job and he took it!" Gloria Robards presented not as a question but as a summation statement. "Figure out what he likes to eat so we can have it in the house."

"Mom," Mae slightly whined. "There's so much happening right now I hardly think that is the priority."

"Mae, meals are always the priority!" Her mother was very decisive on this. Mae shook her head, but she could see Scarpetta looking at her through the rearview in a manner which suggested that she was very much in agreement with Mae's mom.

"Fine. I'll ask," responded Mae, caving to will of the two very passionate ladies.

"Good," her mom said, clearly very happy that Mae had come to her senses. "I don't know why you were making such a big deal out of it. Where are you going to eat tonight?"

"I found a little roadside inn just off the highway in Pennsylvania where people can have their dogs stay with them. There's a diner attached," Mae explained. "I'm planning to head out early in the morning, so we'll be home by the following evening, hopefully."

"Great!" Mae's mother sounded satisfied that everyone was going to be fed. "When you get here, we should watch this movie your dad and I just saw, but I'd like to see again. This lady falls in love with a ghost that she meets at the Rockefeller Christmas Tree Lighting. And you think, oh, these two are NEVER going to be able to make it work. I mean, a lady and a ghost? It's a lot to overcome! Plus, in a city? There's so little space. Maybe in the country I could see it working, but in New York? It's almost unheard of! I get that he's a ghost but she had a VERY small one bedroom. Well, you know, you had one! A one bedroom I mean, not a ghost. Anyway, she gets a Christmas wish and he comes back to life! AND, it turns out he still owns a whole building."

"Of course, he does," Mae said rolling her eyes. Her seriousness quickly broke into an amused laughter and then Gloria Robards started laughing too. "You're unbelievable, Mom! I'll never have to watch a movie again. You should have a summations podcast."

It was dark by the time the two vehicles pulled into the roadside inn. There were LED icicles dripping off the roof and bright blue lights on a Christmas tree out front. The establishment was one-story but it looked like there were rooms around the back as well. A sign advertising *Morgan's Bar & Grill* shared the same lot.

133

Mae opened the door to her Jeep and hopped out with Scarpetta close behind. Both of them were so happy to be done driving for the day that they practically danced around the vehicle stretching their legs. Jack had parked his pickup nearby and was heading over with Sammy, who also seemed to have an added skip to his step from being on solid ground.

"I'll go in and get us room keys. Would you mind walking Scarpetta around with you a few times, please?" Mae asked as she grabbed her bag out of the front seat.

"Yeah, no problem, sounds great. Thank you," Jack responded. They had already decided that Mae was going to pay for the hotel and meals along the drive. Although *they decided* was maybe a slightly incorrect way to describe it, Mae thought. It was more like she had insisted that since room and board were a part of his job that she would be paying. When Jack began to protest Mae had said it was non-negotiable. "Scarpetta," Jack called. Scarpetta looked up at Mae who gave her a nod and then she pranced over to the two guys. Mae smiled as she watched the three of them start the loop around the inn before she headed into the office.

"Welcome, welcome!" A kind faced man greeted Mae as he rose from behind the entry desk. There was an adorable white Christmas tree in one corner and a blue lit menorah in the window. "I'm the owner here, Charles Fraser. Will you be staying for the night?"

"Yes! Thank you. I'm Mae Robards. I have a reservation for two rooms, both with dogs. I called last night." Mae explained.

"Great!" Charles Fraser looked through his registry until he found Mae's name. "Here you are—two rooms, two pooches!"

"Would it be possible to be around back?" Mae asked as she looked at her Jeep packed full of her belongings.

Charles immediately picked up on Mae's worries. "Of course, no problem. We also have cameras in the lot and the only way to get to the back is by driving around the office here. I'm at the desk all night. My wife swaps out with me in the morning."

"I really appreciate it," Mae smiled. She filled out the paperwork and briefly glanced at all the leaflets advertising places to check out in the area. Charles handed Mae keys and informed her that the grill served food until ten pm and was open again at six am for breakfast.

"Perfect!" Mae said. She was so hungry! She thanked Charles and went back out to the parking area where

Jack was still circling with Scarpetta and Sammy close behind. Mae held up the keys, "Shall we take the kids to our respective rooms and meet at the grill for dinner in about fifteen minutes?"

"Sounds good!" Jack headed over and Mae tossed him his key. The two got back in their vehicles, drove around the lot and went to their separate rooms.

Mae was happy to see that they were on opposite sides at the back of the inn. She wasn't sure she was ready to share a wall. She needed a good sleep for the drive tomorrow and felt like having Jack that close could keep a woman up all night. At the thought, Mae shook her head so vigorously that Scarpetta looked over at her with a questioning eye. Mae worried that she was starting to act like she was in a *Twilight* novel. She was an adult! And she most certainly wasn't the type to stay up all night intently listening to how a man slept. Especially not through a wall!

"Pull it together," she told herself in the bathroom mirror. "The only people who listen to other people sleep are serial killers and apnea specialists!" She did a quick brush of the teeth, patted on some under eye concealer and added a dash of mascara. "This is just so I feel refreshed!" She told Scarpetta, who didn't seem to be buying Mae's weak explanation at all, but then again neither was Mae. She put out some water and food for Scarpetta, then headed over to the grill.

Jack was already seated at a booth when Mae arrived and he waved her over. The establishment was done up in little white lights, the glow making their red booths look like holiday magic. Mae could hear Faith Hill singing *Where Are You Christmas?* over the speakers and she tried not to sing along too loudly to the song she loved so very much. Mae was just switching from humming along quietly to breaking into the full-blown chorus when she tripped over a step leading up to the booths. She caught herself and tried to make it look like it was part of a dance move as she continued towards the table and sheepishly slid in across from Jack. He had changed his shirt and his eyes seemed to sparkle in the twinkling lights of the grill. Mae took a sip of the water that was already on the table and mentally admonished herself for thinking about idiotic things like twinkling eyes. She accidentally also thought about how good he must smell and then drank the entire glass of water.

"You must be thirsty?" Jack smiled.

"What? Oh, yeah, I get so dehydrated when I'm driving." Which *was* true, Mae reminded herself, and then immediately started perusing the menu. After a couple of seconds, a waitress came by and refilled their water glasses.

"Shall I give you a few minutes?" she asked. Jack looked at Mae for her answer.

"I'm actually ready. Are you?" Somewhere along the drive Mae had gotten a hankering for an egg salad sandwich and was delighted to see that they had it.

"Shoot," Jack said and gestured that Mae should go first. She ordered her egg salad with fries and a pickle. Jack got a burger, medium rare, and a Caesar salad. They both stuck with water. Mae would have loved to celebrate the end of a long day's journey with a beloved Diet Coke. She always enjoyed the way it kind of burned a person's throat on the way down, as if it was somehow cleansing her from any savage mistakes that she'd made that day. But unfortunately, Mae had been trying to cut down to only drinking three a week, a number she'd already maxed out—in fact, she was pretty sure she her count was currently in the double digits. They drank their water in silence for a few moments, recalibrating from the drive.

"They really did this place up nice!" Mae finally said as she looked around. "Christmas is definitely my most favorite time of the year."

"I can tell!" Jack laughed.

"Runs in the family," Mae explained. "My father is crazy for Christmas."

"Crazy for Christmas! Sounds like the title of a movie that should be on our list."

"It does, doesn't it?" Mae agreed. "My dad and I used to hike into the woods every year to cut down a family tree. I missed it this season but it's one of my absolute favorite traditions. And, he always makes a special roll for Christmas morning that I look forward to. Does your family have any special holiday traditions?" The question just slipped out because Mae was so interested in hearing about Jack's life, but she was immediately worried that since he'd never brought up his family before, that maybe that was too personal.

"My parents…" Jack paused. "My parents died when I was young."

"Oh, Jack, I'm so sorry!" Mae could sense the depth of his loss.

"I appreciate it. It's OK. It was a long time ago. Not that I don't still miss them but…" Jack trailed off as their food arrived. They both thanked the waitress and took a bite of their meals. Mae waited for Jack to continue. "The summer after the accident I got sent to a camp in the woods. I grew up in Colorado, so I've always been surrounded by mountains. Nature was so grounding for me...it really helped me find some kind of peace." Mae nodded thoughtfully and with tremendous care. "I've moved around a lot with different forestry jobs. People who I've worked with have been kind enough to invite me into their homes for the holidays." There was a long pause and Mae realized that Jack was clearly done talking about his childhood. She sat quietly with her egg salad sandwich for a moment.

"Well, we would be delighted to have you spend Christmas with us!" Mae thought her family could probably overwhelm any normal human with their holiday hype, but she knew they'd be happy to have him.

"Thank you. That would be really nice," Jack replied earnestly. "Must be such a big change for you? Going home I mean."

"Yeah. It really hasn't fully hit me yet, I don't think. Seems like a lot at once but I'm hoping we'll figure it all out," Mae grimaced. "The move and I have my book due and then we have to restructure the ski center and drum up some more business. Then I go and invite you to come work with us! You must think I'm slightly haphazard, to say the very least!" Mae tried to laugh but it came out more like panicked air escaping. Another one of her great skill sets was the ability to go emotionally downhill very quickly—it was such a gift, she thought as she exhaled.

"I agreed, didn't I? So at least we'll be reckless together." Jack's smile shined through his eyes and radiated directly into Mae's solar plexus, swinging her mood right back up. How in the absolute heck, Mae questioned herself, was this happening?! But was what she felt even really happening, she wondered? Maybe he was just a man with twinkly eyes and a great toosh who simply was nice, needed an interim gig, and she was reading it totally wrong. "I do really appreciate the offer, Mae." Jack's very serious tone cut through Mae's thoughts. "We were in a rut. I love Rex and Mitzey, but we needed a change. Plus, I can't wait to get a look at your mountains." Mae gulped down another glass of water. "Did you like LA?" He asked seeming not to notice Mae's sudden disorientation.

"I did, I loved it!" Mae looked around for the waitress, she needed more water. "I had never been to the West Coast prior to moving there. Which, just saying that out loud seems like another impulsive decision for my resume, but I mean that worked out so... Anyways! Los Angeles always seemed like a movie set to me. Those palm trees! I'll never get over how cool they look up against the sky."

"The West Coast definitely has some beautiful parks," Jack agreed. The waitress came by, refilled their water glasses, and left. "Must have been a hard change for anyone you may have been dating?"

"Ummm..." Mae couldn't tell if she was blushing. Thank goodness the lighting was low. Hopefully, it just looked like she was still tan from all the LA talk. She could not believe he had asked her about dating. Maybe he wasn't just a man who liked *Lord of the Rings*? Maybe he was also into Mae? Or maybe she was losing her mind. "I wasn't dating anyone seriously. When I'm writing... I call it *going under*," Mae laughed. It sounded so ridiculous when she explained it to someone else. "I'm such a geek! Anyways! When I'm writing, I need to shut myself off for large stretches of time. That doesn't seem to sit well with...with a lot of people."

"I know that feeling," Jack confided.

"Oh?" Mae wondered if he really did know that feeling. It had been her experience that a lot of men thought it was great that she had her own thing going on, but then after not being prioritized, precisely when they wanted to be prioritized, they seemed to feel quite differently about it.

"I also go off for chunks of time with the Forest Service. It seems to have been hard on my…hard on people. As you said," Jack nodded in understanding.

"Yeah. I guess a lot of people need…" Mae didn't know the right words, probably because it was so out of her wheelhouse. "More structured time? Or I guess a regular together schedule?"

"And I can absolutely understand that," Jack jumped in. "People should be able to get what they need from a relationship…some people just need different things."

"I guess, I've just always felt like the odd one out on that," Mae said and took the last bite of her sandwich. Maybe he did have a similar experience she thought. She then suddenly felt emotionally naked and abruptly decided to change the subject. "So! You are about to enter Robards' Christmas Country! Do you have any favorite foods or cookies or soups or anything? My mom wants to know."

"Your mom, huh?" Jack went easily with the change in topic.

"Yeah, she centers a lot of conversations around food," Mae explained.

"Probably her way of showing love," said Jack. The comment took Mae aback slightly. She hadn't thought of it that way. She'd always felt like it was her mom changing the subject or focusing on something else, but Mae could see how it might be her mom's way of wanting to take care of everyone. "Well!" Jack continued. "I love all soups except for split pea. In fact, I don't like pea anything. I love stuffing, and sweet potatoes, and green beans. Oh, and of course, ALL the cookies."

"Sounds like a great list!" Mae enthused. "In your travels, have you ever had a Needham?"

"A need-who?" Jack asked so seriously that it made Mae giggle.

"A Needham. It's a traditional New England homemade candy. It's a bit of mashed potatoes mixed with coconut and then dipped in dark chocolate," Mae explained. She loved Needhams so much that she rarely made them as it was too hard not to eat the entire batch at once.

"Potatoes, wow! I didn't see that coming. And I should have...because potatoes have eyes." Jack raised his brows. The puns were back.

"Oh! No!" Mae would have been mortified if she hadn't found it to be the cutest thing ever. Which she concluded, that realization itself, was even more mortifying.

"Don't get mashed up about it!" Jack's puns had taken off running.

"Uh-oh...ummm...." Mae's brain went blank for a second as she mentally scrolled through potato words. What was this delightfully weird thing happening to her, she wondered briefly before coming to one, "I've never had TUBOR-culosis." As soon as it came out of her mouth Mae squinted recognizing that one was pretty far off the rails.

"Ha! What?!" Jack almost spit out his water. "You really took a left there. But hey, I guess you gotta HASH it out."

"What can I tell ya? I'm half baked." Mae was back in it. "I'm fried, you wanna head out?"

"Yeah, let's scallop out of here... Scallop. Gallop. Like scalloped potatoes? Or maybe it sounds more like skiddadle? Scallapple?" As Jack worked out the best exit potato reference, Mae politely waved for the check. She was grinning ear to ear. You gotta reel this in, she thought, you have some deeply ROOTED problems. Then she eye-rolled herself.

Chapter 11 - The Cross Country Ski Center (A Second 'Cross Country' Reference Oh My!)

The following day they had woken up at sunrise, walked the dogs, grabbed a breakfast sandwich and coffee (of course Mae had already drunk the entire pot in her room), and headed back out on the road. It had been smooth driving the whole way up. But, as New Hampshire drew closer and closer, Mae found herself focusing in on all that had to get done. She pushed away thoughts from the previous evening about the walk back to their rooms when they'd been standing so close that the clouds of air from their breath had joined in between them. Mae had turned away first, reminding Jack (and herself), that they had an early morning. She had tried to throw in a potato latke reference by making it sound like *lotta,* but either Jack hadn't heard it, or it was so bad that even he had to pretend it hadn't happened. Mae didn't know how to process all the Jack feelings, so instead she focused on brainstorming alternative twists for her book. She still felt that something was not right about the current story arc. It needed something extra, something unforeseen. She also thought about her parents and what they needed to do immediately in order to stay open until

Mae had more time to help. She looked at Scarpetta through the rearview and declared, "It's going to be OK. We will be OK." Scarpetta looked back at her comfortably, clearly totally relaxed about the situation. At least one of them was, Mae thought.

It was just after sundown when Mae and Jack drove into The Robards' Cross Country Ski Center. The family home was on the same lot and the trails were hidden away in the beautiful woods out back. Mae pulled up to the house and parked. Jack pulled in next to her. They both were exiting their vehicles when Mae's parents came out the front, the light from inside spilling out the door with them onto yard.

There was some snow on the ground but it was not a lot. Usually, they got the bulk of their snow after Christmas, during the months of January and February, and sometimes through March and April depending. The Robards' had invested in some minor snowmaking equipment when it had become more readily available for smaller businesses, but it was an incredible amount of work and only took place at nighttime when temps were coldest. They had to lug the equipment around and usually just ended up letting all the artificial snow pile up in the open field by the lake at the center of the property, instead of trying to drag the hose and compressor along the slim trails in the woods. And then, with a combination that almost seemed like a dance, they would plow and/or drag the snow onto enough of the main course to stay open until the real deal snow fell later in the season. Mae looked past the house into the dark woods. She loved it back there, especially when it was snowing. It was simply magical.

Her parents hurried over and wrapped Mae up in a big hug. She hugged them back, hard. It did feel good to be home. Scarpetta jumped on the back of Mae's legs, wanting in on it too. Kurt Robards bent down to give the pooch the ear rub she loved so much.

"Mom, Dad, this is Jack Wilder!" Mae introduced them, recognizing how absolutely crazy it was that she was bringing this man that she had just met home. Then she reminded herself that they had to hire someone, and most likely it would've been a friend of a friend anyway, so why not Jack?! "Jack these are my parents, Gloria and Kurt Robards." Mae's mother was originally from Hawaii and was quite possibly one of the tallest people in the entire state of New Hampshire. Kurt Robards, on the other hand, was not only born and raised in New Hampshire, but his parents were too, as were their parents before. It was quite plausible that the Robards' family line literally sprung from the mountains.

"Mrs. Robards. Mr. Robards. Great to meet you!" Jack shook both their hands warmly.

"Call me Gloria," Mae's mother beamed.

"And Kurt," her dad followed.

"And, over there being a shy guy…" Jack pointed to his pup who'd been hanging back by the wheel of the truck. "Is Samwise, I call him Sammy for short. He's a little bit timid with new people." They all looked at Sammy and then turned to see Scarpetta, who, in contrast, was running around them in circles and playing in the light snow.

"She's working on him," Mae smiled at the dogs.

"Not a wicked ton of snow out front," explained Mae's dad to Jack. "But we have enough on the trails for our yearly regulars who've already been coming to do some skiing. It will be nice when we get a good storm though."

"You kids must be tired from all the driving. We're making dinner," said Gloria Robards, deftly maneuvering the conversation to food. "Let's get Jack settled in, and then we'll eat."

"And then maybe we can squeeze in a Christmas movie," Kurt added hopefully and then directed his attention back to Jack. "Did Mae mention to you that I'm a huge Christmas fan?"

"It's possible that was mentioned," Jack responded jovially as he grabbed a couple bags out of the back of his truck.

"Jack, obviously, if you want to acclimate on your own time you don't have to eat with us…if you have other plans or whatever," said Mae not wanting to over-Robards the man too soon. The three of them were a whole lotta Christmas at once for someone who was unfamiliar.

"Like, if I have a night on the town planned?" Jack joked. "I'd love to join you all for dinner. Thank you."

"Let's show Jack the cabin then!" Mae's mother beamed a little too broadly for Mae's comfort. "Can we help you with your bags?"

"I don't have a lot of stuff," Jack explained rather sheepishly.

"I think Mae has enough for everyone!" At Gloria Robards' words they all turned to look at Mae's Jeep which was packed to the brim. "You should see how much she shipped, oh my goodness gracious me!"

"OK, OK! Mom! Considering that's like fifteen years of stuff, I think I did pretty reasonably," Mae retorted defensively.

"Well, I've been putting A LOT of your shipped boxes in the backroom," her mom said as if she was filing a complaint in small claims court.

"You both did great!" Kurt Robards stepped in before the conversation went somewhere unreasonable. "Let's show Jack the back cabin." They all grabbed things out of the truck and led Jack towards the ski center where the cabin stood out back. Scarpetta danced out in front of them, as if leading the way, while Sammy hesitantly took up the rear like he was watching for anything suspicious.

"Inside there is the office for the ski touring center. It has a large entry room and lockers for people to leave their stuff," Gloria explained, pointing out details as they went. "We can show you everything another day! Then around back we have a separate living quarters." Their tour group came around the side of the building and arrived at the cutest little cabin. "Your father put up some extra lights."

"Oh, it looks great dad!" Mae exclaimed. She admired the beautifully hung lights intermixed with some bows. Her father had really done quite the holiday job.

"We don't often lock doors around here Jack, but here's the key just in case," Kurt said as he reached into his pocket and handed Jack a collection of keys. "The office center ones are also on there. There's a fireplace in the cabin. I took the liberty of starting a fire already for this evening. Wood is on the other side under a tarp. If it drops below thirty-two degrees inside the oil heat will automatically come on so the pipes don't start to freeze," Mae's dad explained.

"OK, let's leave Jack to it then!" Mae wanted to let him have a moment of privacy upon seeing his new place. His new *temporary* place, she corrected, wanting to remind herself that this was just a transitional thing. They all put down the boxes and bags that they were carrying on the small wooden porch.

"If you have any questions, or need anything else, please let us know. Oh, and that's the house over there!" Gloria said as she pointed, back in tour-guiding mode. "Dinner will probably be ready in about thirty minutes, if you want to head over then." Her mother was smiling so hard at Jack that Mae wanted to physically haul her off.

"Tomorrow, I'll take you into town so you can see the sights and get the lay of the land, if you want," Mae said as she tried to shoo her parents back towards the house. "OK, so that's that! Let's let him have some space guys. And I have to go unload the Jeep." Mae stepped off the cabin steps.

"Do you want any help?" Jack offered. Her mom beamed again. Dang it, mom, thought Mae, let's all act like we've been here before.

"I'm good, but thanks so much for asking," Mae replied. "You just do you, get settled. We'll be in the house if you need anything." Mae then practically dragged her parents back towards the parking lot.

"Seems like a very solid and nice guy," said her dad when they are almost to the Jeep.

"Yes, and QUITE handsome," added Gloria.

"MOM!" exclaimed Mae looking around to make sure that they were well out of ear shot. "Come on! I didn't notice."

"You didn't notice, HA! Mae Robards, you don't fool me one bit!" Her mom smacked her bum and then they all took to unloading the Jeep.

An hour later they were all seated around the table just finishing dinner, which had been absolutely amazing. Mae was reminded of her deep gratitude for home cooked meals. Her parents had really pulled out all the stops for them tonight. Mae usually cooked for herself but often it was a mishmash of what was essentially the condiments she had left in her fridge.

"This was so delicious! Thank you," said Jack as he cleared his plate from the table.

"Our pleasure!" Gloria couldn't have been happier.

"We're a pretty big cooking family here Jack," Kurt explained in case anyone had missed it. "And whenever we aren't eating or cooking, we like to be discussing what we should plan to have next!" He let out deep chuckle and patted his wife's arm.

"I put some dog treats in the pantry if you want to try and give Sammy one?" Mae said as she turned her attention to the pup, who was still essentially hiding in the corner. Mae recognized that new places could be daunting and usually nothing greased the wheel like a little extra food. Worked for her more often than not.

"Try to bribe Sammy more like," Jack added as Mae brought out the doggie treats and handed them over.

Both dogs immediately perked up, totally in tune to the comings and goings of food in the room. Mae gave Scarpetta an eyeball and looked over at Sammy.

Scarpetta seemed to recognize what was happening and settled back down to wait her turn. She's a better woman than me, Mae thought to herself about her wonderfully patient pooch.

"Samwise… Comeer boy! Samwise. Sammy!" Jack coaxed the pup to come join the group with the promise of a treat held in his hands. Slowly and shyly, Sammy loped over and delicately took the treat from Jack. The group cheered and it looked to Mae that even Scarpetta seemed proud.

"Samwise huh?" Kurt turned to Jack. "I'm sure Mae has told you that she's also a huge fan of *The Lord of the Rings.* Around here we actually just refer to it as *The Trilogy.*" Mae's dad brought out the air quotes for that one.

"No…in fact, she didn't mention it," Jack grinned. "Very interesting." He turned to Mae who turned to face the pantry, as if it was suddenly so interesting that she just had to look inside it at that exact moment.

"Oh, didn't I?" Mae muttered.

"Anytime Mae is upset she watches all three of them back-to-back!" Kurt Robards was giving up all her *LOTR* secrets.

"Now that's a commitment!" Jack was seemingly psyched about the news.

"Well, sometimes…" Mae said fixing her shirt as if she was about to present to the court. "Sometimes I just watch the second half of *Two Towers*. If there are time constraints."

"Seems logical," Jack smiled. "The part where Gandalf shows up at the top of the mountain?"

"Yes!" Mae agreed enthusiastically. There was no way to tone down her Gandalf love so why was she bothering to hold back. "Right when he said he was going to!" She was getting so pumped all over again, she could watch it again right now! Or even re-enact the entire thing, as she knew it all by heart. And mayyyyybe had her own cloak.

"Followed up by that Samwise Gamgee speech…" Sammy lifted his head hearing Jack say his name.

"YES!" Mae said even louder this time. It was her favorite part. "It's almost like a Rocky montage; I get so worked up!" Mae was beyond thrilled but then she caught a glimpse of her parents smiling at her and immediately went back to looking in the pantry.

"Since we are on the topic of a movie…" her dad began seizing his moment. "How about a Christmas flick?" Everyone agreed that a movie would be lovely, and after finishing clearing the table, they made their way into the living room to close out the night.

Mae's mom and dad were seated on the couch with Mae and Jack settled in the big comfy chairs on either side. The two dogs were laying around the Christmas tree at the opposite end of the room by the big windows that faced towards the back woods. The fire was crackling, and Mae felt so warm and relaxed that for a moment she started to worry that she should try to be more anxious. The group decided on a new streaming holiday movie that no one had seen yet. Watching a movie with the Robards was an experience unto itself. Mae's mother loved to do a running narrative over any movie and Mae found it to be charmingly hilarious but also slightly mortifying as she stole glimpses at Jack's expressions.

"Kurt, where do we know that guy from?" Gloria asked her husband. It was her usual intro question. "Was he in M.A.S.H.?" No one seemed to know. Mae let her mom know that her phone was charging in the other room but that she would google the actor's name later. "Did she just walk into that house and leave the door open? Who does that?" Mae's mom hated that people had to edit films. She wanted to see everything. "How come people never excuse themselves to use the facilities in movies? It isn't normal!" On that comment, Mae stared up at the ceiling trying to stifle a laugh, unbelievable.

The Holiday Breakdown

Chapter 12 - Trim that Tree

Friday morning proved to be a crisp and sunny beautiful day in Snow Creek. Mae had driven Jack into town. They were walking down the main street so Mae could point out all the whats and wheres. The small village, which was nestled in the northern foothills of the White Mountains, seemed to be done up entirely in Christmas.

"So, this is our town," Mae said to Jack as she pointed out the grocer and the Post Office.

"Snow Creek," Jack said and did a full three sixty turn taking in the area.

"Snow Creek," Mae repeated as she breathed in a deep gulp of the clean air.

"It's very picturesque," Jack responded admiring his surroundings.

"We are cute!" Mae agreed.

"Yeah, you are," Jack said as he turned to face Mae on the sidewalk. Was he talking about the town, or was he talking about Mae? She couldn't tell, but her windpipe seemed to suddenly have something stuck in it. There was a very long pause as Mae tried to keep her mouth shut, a feat she normally found to be almost impossible, but it looked like Jack was about to say something else and she was pretty sure that she wanted to hear it.

"There you are!" A voice suddenly came from behind Mae which she recognized immediately, not only from the timbre, but by the accompanying wonderful smell of Angel perfume that enveloped her. Her best friend from growing up, Renee Donato, had been wearing that perfume ever since it came out when they were in middle school. Delighted, Mae turned around and found herself wrapped in the warm hug of her friend. "I called the ski center to see if you were back yet and your mom said you were in town," Renee explained.

"Renee, this is Jack Wilder," said Mae stepping back to introduce the two. "Jack's a Forest Ranger who's off for the season currently and has kindly agreed to help us maintain the trails for the time being. Jack, this is my friend, Renee Donato. She owns the bakery down the street, AND, on the flip side of the building, facing the other road, is also Renee's gym." Mae explained, so proud of her friend.

"I call them both my buns businesses!" Renee laughed. *"Renee's Buns I & II!"*

"Ha! Great!" Jack immediately took to Renee and her fun word play. "Gotta get your customers from all angles!"

"YES!" Renee cheered wholeheartedly. "Do you guys have time to swing by? Tim is working and would love to see you, Mae. Plus, we just might have something freshly baked for you." Tim was Renee's eldest son. Mae had been there when he was born because Renee's husband hadn't been able to get back from overseas while working for the Armed Forces. Mae was living in NYC for college at that point, and upon receiving Renee's nervous message she'd immediately hopped into her car and made it just in time to be there for her friend. Renee's husband, Rob (who Mae had also known in high school as Renee and Rob were teenage sweethearts—although he was from as few towns over so Renee's mom had then categorized it as a "long distance relationship"), had made it back shortly after the birth. He was currently overseas again working as a civilian for the Navy, but luckily for everyone involved, he had been back for the birth of his other two children. Renee and Rob had quite possibly the most well-behaved children Mae had ever met, and she always appreciated how the five of them made it all work.

"Yes, I'd love to come by! If that's ok with you Jack?" Mae asked, realizing that she didn't want him to feel dragged along.

"Who could say no to fresh baked goods?!" Jack smiled and the three of them cheerfully made their way down the street.

"How are the girls?" Mae asked Renee about her two younger daughters.

"They're good!" Renee responded happily as she led them towards her building. "Both are over at their grandma's getting ready for Christmas."

A cheerful bell dinged as the group opened the door into the bright and warm bakery. Mae was immediately greeted by the wonderful smell of sugary dough. She took in a deep breath and felt like she could taste the sweetness in the air. Tim was standing behind a glass counter that housed the baskets of baked goods.

"Tim!" Mae exclaimed as she went for a hug. "Looks as though you're taking over the bakery, huh?!" Tim blushed, deeply.

"This is my eldest," Renee explained to Jack. "We're trying him out over the winter holidays behind the counter. It will be Tim's first Christmas selling buns!

"MOM!" Tim blushed again.

"Tim, this is Jack. He's in town for a while helping us out at the ski center with the trails," Mae explained.

"Mom said you were moving back."

"Yeah, I am…or, I guess, I did." Mae caught herself forgetting again that all her stuff was now here. Her life was now back here.

"Well! We're all so happy to have you home," Renee said as she rubbed Mae's shoulders in a comforting manner. "AND, in your honor we made a special batch of your favorite chocolate crullers today. Tim, let's heat one of those up for Mae." She moved from addressing her son to addressing Jack. "What would you like? It's on the house!"

"Oh, thank you!" Jack said gratefully as he perused the blackboard menu on the wall. "I guess I'll do a chocolate cruller as well, but everything definitely looks great."

"Tim, make it two crullers please, and how about you warm us up one of the new Christmas muffins you created. We'll all share it." Then, as if in secret conference with her friend, Renee added, "Tim is becoming a bit of a baker extraordinaire."

"MOM!" Tim exclaimed again, as Renee's whispers travelled to his ears. He got to working on the items and

Renee stepped around the register to put together a coffee tray for everyone. Mae had always admired how cute Renee was able to make everything look without going as far as making a person want to throw up. It was like she knew exactly where the line was between a*wwwwwww* and *what the heck happened here?!*

Renee led the way over to one of the darling tables where she laid down the tray of coffee and put out cups for everyone. Tim came over moments shortly thereafter with a plate of treats.

"It all looks so delicious, thank you," Mae said as she smiled up at Tim. Renee beamed and touched her son's arm proudly.

"MOM!" Tim exclaimed again. He slunk away from the table pretending to be embarrassed but clearly feeling very good about his work.

"We're so proud of him," Renee confided as soon as Tim turned the corner and headed into the back. "You never know what your kids are going to take to and he just loves baking. And, he's VERY good at it, and I'm not just saying that. I wouldn't."

"Oh, I know you wouldn't," Mae agreed emphatically. She knew Renee to be a very upbeat and positive person but had also been on the other end of

Renee's truth telling on many an occasion. Mae actually really appreciated that about her friend because she always knew exactly where she stood and what Renee really thought about things. Mae found that to be very comforting. Mae had also learned very early on not to ask Renee anything that she didn't want a real answer to. The two friends then laughed in the shared knowledge of Renee's renowned directness.

"This is delicious!" Jack piped in after taking a bite of the Christmas muffin. He raised his voice a little louder to make sure Tim could hear him. "My compliments to the Head Baker." The bell on the door suddenly rang again as Derek Mumford walked in, and Mae was reminded of what an incredibly small town (and world) it was.

"The man himself!" Derek pronounced, as he turned and beelined towards the table greeting his friend. He smiled broadly at Jack. His face was reddened from years spent on windy mountaintops. "Jack Wilder! When you asked about the Robards and they asked about you, I thought I might be seeing you soon!" He gave his friend a strong hug.

"Derek and Jack worked together on a forestry job in Alaska," Mae explained to Renee.

"Small world," Renee winked, reiterating Mae's feelings exactly.

"Isn't it?!" said Derek in a tone that seemed to match Renee's wink.

"Jack's going to help us with the trails until he finds a new placement," Mae said, outlining the plan. She was suddenly feeling very self-conscious and like she should explain the business situation at hand. "Brian had to leave last minute."

"I heard," Derek replied, still smiling too hard. Mae took that moment to have more of the amazing cruller and to look down at her plate so she didn't have to make eye contact with Jack.

"I have your order, Mr. Mumford," Tim announced as he came out from that back balancing a bunch of boxes tied with red strings.

"For the family Christmas party," Derek disclosed to Mae and Jack. "It was great to see you. I'm sure we'll all be seeing each other again soon." Derek turned and headed towards the counter to pay. "Thanks so much Tim! Such a festive looking haul."

"Here, let me help you carry some of those to your car Derek," Jack said as he jumped up to join his friend.

"Ladies, I'll be right back." He grabbed a few of the bakery boxes and headed out the door with Derek.

"It'd be nice to dash through that snow," Renee said in a conspiratorial tone as soon as the two men had exited the bakery and could be seen walking down the sidewalk, presumably towards Derek's vehicle.

"Yeah, I would really like to trim that tree!" Mae responded instantly in her most *tell me about it* manner before catching herself. "I mean, come on Renee! He's here to help with the trails. I just met him! He was out of work and needed a…"

"I think the lady dost protest too much!" Renee laughed and then switched tones looking at her friend. "I know it's a lot happening all at once for you. Deciding to come back after all these years. Figuring out how to make it all work. If you need me, you know I'm here, for whatever."

"Thanks Renee, I really appreciate it." Mae took a beat. "I swing back and forth from feeling like this is so right to loud voices in my head screaming, WHAT ARE YOU DOING?! I'm still stuck on my new book. I just can't seem to finish it! I get mad at myself when I'm not working on it, but I know from the past that it often takes me stepping away, and then it all just comes at once. Oh, and I didn't tell you this yet, there's a new editor and I gotta say, she's a real downer. Plus, I INVITED A MAN I JUST MET back to New Hampshire like I'm some kind of a Hallmark Betty!" Mae shook her head and took another bite of the chocolate cruller. It was incredibly tasty, and somehow very reassuring; amazing how warm chocolate could do that.

"You are a Hallmark Betty, Mae, don't kid yourself. You adore those movies. You're like half Hallmark Betty and half punk rock. That's what I love about you!" Renee put her arm around her friend's shoulder. "You're doing great! And, I'm betting that during one of your walks out on trails the perfect words to finish your book will just jump right out at you. In the meantime, practically magically, you happen to have a handsome, almost stranger here who can help you with the ski center AND he knows someone you know, so he's at least fifty percent not a murderer. I would actually give it sixty percent. Those are pretty good odds!" Renee winked for the second time. "It's also possible that the new editor will be overcome with holiday spirit and stop being a poophat! Unlikely yes, but still possible."

"You can be so positive!" Mae laughed and sort of groaned at the same time.

"And you can be so not! I like that about us." Renee finished off the Christmas muffin.

"I'm positive!" Mae protested. "I just like to cover all the vast possibilities." The two friends started laughing again just as Jack turned back towards the bakery.

"Speaking of vast possibilities," Renee intoned in her best vavavoom voice.

"MOM!" Mae repeated Tim's embarrassed mantra.

The Holiday Breakdown

Chapter 13 - Actually, Just Like the Prime Minister

The next morning Mae was upstairs in her old room, which, she corrected herself again, was her now her new room. They'd temporarily put most of the belongings she'd brought back from LA in the garage, otherwise the room would have been wall-to-wall box. Mae wasn't even going to try to start to unpack and figure out where things should go until after her draft was done. Although she had been managing to write every night, she still had the feeling that something was off and hadn't yet figured out exactly what it was. Mae was planning on taking the day to lock herself in and focus, but first she was going to show Jack the trails. Yesterday, after returning from Renee's bakery, Jack, Mae, and her parents had taken the afternoon to set up a part-time work schedule that was good for everyone and to talk over the different aspects of trail maintenance. This morning Mae was going to meet up with Jack over at the ski center to give him the full tour. Then, her father, who had just headed out to get extra sand buckets for the driveway, would show Jack how the snow machine worked when he returned. But, at this moment, Mae was particularly excited about showing Jack the woods.

Mae looked in her closet to see what choices she had for snow pants. She still owned a full onesie from when she was younger. It was black and orange with a ridiculous metal clasp belt and Mae absolutely loved it. Luckily for Mae, she'd had a huge growth spurt at a very young age, so although it was rough as a teenager to look taller and older than everyone, she could still fit into a lot of her high school clothes. Unfortunately, it wasn't quite cold enough to wear it yet so Mae decided on a pair of wind pants and gators. All her winter gear was still in its place from when she was home last Christmas and had helped out on the trails, but this year it was a different feeling entirely. This year she was no longer visiting. Mae was pulling the wind pants on over her leggings, thinking about the huge change, when her phone beeped. Mae glanced at her cell to see that it was a text from Julie with a link to a video:

New Christmas song out. Thought of you! Love Love Love!

Mae popped in her earbuds and clicked on the video. It was a singer that Mae hadn't heard of before, but then again, Mae hadn't heard of a lot people. Her go-to music playlists were always either 90s pop or 70s classic rock or, of course, Christmas music. The uplifting beat filled

Mae's ears and she immediately loved it. The song fulfilled all the quintessential holiday music lyric requirements: fireplaces, hot beverages, snowflakes, walking hand in hand, and Santa. Mae loved it so much that she finished dressing and decided to play it again. Keeping the earbuds in, she grabbed a jacket and danced out into the hall. Mae shimmied over to the backup winter closet where the Robards kept extra mittens and hats and grabbed some warm work gloves for herself and for Jack. She continued the dance down the stairs and moonwalked into the kitchen, shaking her bum to the fun Christmas beat. When the chorus came around again Mae was in full swing and did a dramatic spin imitating a professional figure skater. When she put her toe down to stop herself from toppling over, she looked up and her mouth immediately went dry. There was Jack, standing in the kitchen, smiling broadly. Mae pulled the earbuds out and her eyes widened so big she was afraid they might fall from of her head. Scarpetta, who was over by the fireplace, made a bit of a whining noise that sounded to Mae like it could almost be a giggle.

"Sorry, I ran into your mom out front who was heading out to volunteer at the Church Food Pantry and she asked if I could return these to the house," Jack said holding up a pile of recyclable bags. "I tried to yell up, but I guess you didn't hear me because of the earphones." He was very clearly trying to stifle a laugh as Mae took a beat just to stare blindly into the depths of mortification.

"Let's go see the trails then!" Mae decided it was best to act like nothing had happened. Her entire being reddened with embarrassment thinking about how long Jack had been standing there. But she put on her winter hat, slapped a pair of the gloves into Jack's hands and marched straight out the door.

It took only moments for Mae to forget how appalled she felt as she quickly became immersed in the joy that she got from walking out on the back trails. The Robards kept a packed down snowmobile path for walking that was only a few feet away from the main lanes so there would never be any footprints on the ski tracks themselves. It was so incredibly peaceful out in the woods. Mae loved the way the tree branches danced in the light wind. Her absolute favorite time to be out there was when it was snowing or just after a snowstorm when she would get to break fresh tracks. It always reminded Mae of *Whoville* from *How the Grinch Stole Christmas,* with the marshmallow snow tops blanketing everything that a person could see. Plus, right after a new snow, the air glowed and Mae always felt surrounded by a quiet soothing light. It could only be described as magical.

Currently, there was snow on the ground, a mix of manmade and real. It was patchy in some areas, and like her dad had said, it would be great when they got a good storm. The dogs had been left by the fireplace for this outing so Mae and Jack could focus on the whats and hows of the trails, but she had promised to take them out again later. Mae explained to Jack about keeping the trails free of debris and cutting back the branches in certain areas.

"I usually do this bit on skis. I'll just go around seeing if anything needs to be cut back or thrown off the trail. You can ski in the tracks, walk on the path or snowmobile. Have you done a lot of cross country skiing?" Mae asked Jack, realizing it was probably a question that should have come up earlier. Although, in her defense, there were many ways to get around the area, but she was irritated with herself that she didn't even know if he enjoyed it.

"I've done some, but not as much as I'd like to. Looks like now is the perfect opportunity. Seems like a dream, being out here whooshing through the woods." Jack stopped walking and turned to look out past the tracks back into the forest. "It's just so peaceful."

"Isn't it?" Mae gazed out with Jack into the beautiful wilderness. After a moment of allowing her mind to get lost in the incredible landscape, Mae realized that their breathing was in sync. All of a sudden it seemed like they were standing extremely close. Mae's hands started to sweat under her gloves. Jack turned to her, seemingly about to say something, when all of a sudden, the sound of skis sliding through the snow met Mae's ears. She looked towards the trail that was running over a little hill just beyond them as a figure came gliding down.

"Mae!" Reverend Woods pulled to a stop, stuck her poles in the ground, pushed back her goggles and wrapped Mae in a big hug. "I figured since your mom was heading over to watch The Church Food Pantry that I would come out here and get a little nature for my soul. It is glorious!" The Reverend smiled deeply as her face seemed to light up on the word *glorious*. "It's so great to have you home. Our Mae!" She clasped Mae's hands. "And you must be Jack." She turned her smile at the man standing by Mae's side. "I heard you were friends with Derek Mumford and met our Mae when her Jeep broke down on the drive home. Angels among us I tell you!"

"How did you..." Mae reddened, thinking about how Reverend Woods already knew all the goings on when she had barely been home two days!

"Oh, the whole town is talking about it, Mae!" Reverend Woods said, totally delighted.

"The whole town?" Mae turned a deeper shade.

"Practically a Christmas miracle, isn't it? Brian had to leave and then you meet Jack?! Incredible one might say." The Reverend glowed and Mae tried to hide in her hat, appalled at the thought of being the center of town gossip.

"One might!" Jack agreed, laughing.

"Reverend Woods let's not embarrass anyone, oh my goodness!" Mae wanted to run out into the trees and get lost for eternity. She wondered if there was ever going to be a moment in her life when she would come off as cool and unaffected. But sadly, she already knew the answer to her own question, no, no there wouldn't be.

"I'm not embarrassed," replied Jack, his smiling eyes looking back and forth between both women.

"Oh, Mae loves to be embarrassed!" Reverend Woods said, embarrassing Mae further. "She was always so serious with the wearing all black and reading detective books at such a young age. Walking around pretending she was Sherlock Holmes. But underneath it all, our Mae is a total moosh." Mae flinched, pulled her hat down even further and squinted, searching for a cave somewhere in the forest that she could crawl into and hide until spring.

"A moosh even?!" Jack was enjoying this, for whatever reason Mae did not know.

"Did she tell you about the time she showed up to school dressed as a wizard detective?" The Reverend was relentless. "Oh my! It was so delightful."

"No, I don't believe that was ever mentioned," Jack said, giving Mae a *do-tell* kind of a look. "A wizard detective? Fantastic!"

"Ok! Ok! Ok! Let's not wander any further down adolescent memory lane, shall we?" Mae was one quarter laughing, three quarters mortified.

"Will I be seeing you all at the Christmas Eve service?" Reverend Woods deftly changed topics, clearly not meaning to make Mae feel so self-conscious.

"They have THE most beautiful service," Mae exclaimed, delighted to talk about something else. "At the end we light candles, turn off the lights and sing *Silent Night.* It's gorgeous."

"It is so serene," Reverend Woods agreed. "A few times it has even started snowing right as we exited the Church and walked out into Christmas Eve."

"Obviously, no pressure to come Jack," Mae jumped in not wanting him to feel obligated. "But you are welcome."

"Most welcome," the Reverend beamed. "Also, I'm sure Mr. Robards will try to cajole you into a few of the family Christmas traditions." She redirected to Mae. "Has your dad started making his famous Christmas rolls yet?"

"Not yet," Mae replied.

"Well, I always look forward to mine, immensely." She smiled a not-so-subtle smile. "Hint, hint." The Revered winked, pulled her goggles back on and grabbed her poles. "Very nice to meet you, Jack. And Mae, so delighted to have you home." At that she waved and whooshed off.

"I can't wait to try some of these Christmas rolls I keep hearing about," Jack said as he turned to Mae. "You guys really do it up."

"We do indeed," Mae agreed. She took a brief moment and then added, "Sorry about that Jack."

"About what?" He asked, seeming genuinely not to know what she was referring to.

"About everyone in town being up in your business." Mae said feeling dumber by the minute.

"I don't mind," Jack replied earnestly. "It seems nice."

"I don't want you to think…" Mae trailed off. She felt embarrassed because the entire town was enjoying the odd transpiring of events that had brought Mae and Jack to Snow Creek. She was starting to feel incredibly vulnerable because he was learning so much about her and about her family. She felt excited when she was with him, and that in itself was starting to deeply worry Mae. What if it was nothing more than a friendly work relationship? What if he had shared the things with her about his life solely because he thought Mae was a nice person? Here she was giggling about puns and dorky wizard stories while maybe they were just going to be buddies. She was feeling like some giddy teenager and perhaps Jack was just a polite man. Did the entire town, him included, think that Mae was being foolish? It would be too much for her to take. In that moment, Mae realized how hard she was falling for Jack and decided that she just couldn't let that happen. Not now.

"You don't want me to think what?" Jack's question interrupted Mae's thought spiral. There was no way to explain it without admitting how she felt, and Mae most certainly was not going to put herself in that position. What *was* she thinking?! Especially when she should be writing! She reprimanded herself inwardly. She knew better than this!

"Nothing," Mae responded. "OK, well, I should go back and try to get some writing done."

"All right. I'll walk the trails some more until your dad comes home and can show me the equipment. I'm really looking forward to it. I've never made snow!" Jack's excitement made Mae's heart hurt. She didn't want to pretend this was going to be something if it wasn't. She already liked him too much and it had to stop here. She was grateful he was into all the things at the ski center but it seemed more likely than not that those things didn't include Mae personally.

"Sounds good. Thank you," Mae said in a perfectly polite and friendly voice before she turned and walked back in the direction of the house. She decided it would be better if she focused her energy elsewhere to stop herself from falling any further.

Chapter 14 - The Breakdown II

Mae was in her room agonizing over her plot line. Something felt amiss. She would type out a few sentences, get up, walk around, sit down, delete at least half of what she had written and then the process would start all over again. Scarpetta laid on the floor nearby and watched as her human sat and circled, circled and sat. The room was full of tension masked by the smell of balsam candles. Mae always lit a 3-wick when she wrote. If she was to ever make her own line, she'd name each candle with the actual scent and the feeling she was trying to dilute with said candle: Snickerdoodle & Seasonal Depression, Christmas Cookie & Fear of Failure, Balsam & Burgeoning Self Doubt, and so on. Mae was quite enjoying pondering potential existential crisis candle names when she was abruptly brought back to the moment by the stark realization that the one person who wouldn't appreciate these scents was Elizabeth Birk. With that thought, Mae sighed and sat back down at her desk. She stared at the last words she'd written. She stared for so long that her eyesight started to blur.

After much time had passed, Scarpetta got up and came over to give Mae a sniff, presumably thinking that she'd been turned into a statue. Mae suddenly closed out of her document and opened the browser. She looked around the room as if someone might be watching as she cautiously clicked on the search window. As her hesitant manner suggested, Mae knew she was about to do something that was very ill advised. Mae had gone down some very bad spirals on the internet. She actually had to block herself from visiting any sites where people looked up health symptoms; Mae found that you could go in with a headache and come out with meningitis. Self-diagnosing always gave Mae a rash, which she, of course, would then also have to google. It was a never-ending circle of hypochondria.

But Mae's biggest internet problem was reading book reviews, of her books specifically. It never helped her feel better. In fact, it reliably made her feel worse. Mae rarely did it, but for some horrible reason, today was the day that she decided to give it another go. Mae went straight to one of the biggest reviews cites and typed in her name. Her book series immediately popped up. There were many five-star reviews, which Mae scrolled by clearly looking to punish herself. She kept scrolling until three negative reviews popped up. Three in a row! The words reverberated through Mae's head. She read the first one which was accompanied by a one-star rating:

Mae Robards is no Arthur Conan Doyle.

Mae grimaced but firmly reminded herself that no one was and that was the beauty of writing, everyone got to have their own voice.

"Maybe I just need a good detective hat," Mae said to Scarpetta, trying to bring some levity to the situation; a levity that was not going to be reached if she continued to read the reviews, she reminded herself. But she continued on anyway. The next negative review was a slight advancement as it had a two-star rating, so technically, she thought, I've doubled in good since the last one. It read:

The silly meanderings of the first-person voice under cuts the gravitas of the mystery genre.

Mae sat all the way back in her chair on that one. Wow, she thought, was Elizabeth Birk writing these?! The comment picked away at the part of Mae that wanted to be seen as *a real writer*. It also reminded her of how people rarely gave *Best Actor* to a comedic performance and that somehow as a culture we've found that things that are playful are somehow less than. And, that it's often topics that have been deemed *for women* or *by women,* that somehow get looked down upon in this way. Heavens forbid we discuss things that affect us, Mae thought. This was a mental mind cave Mae had blacked out in before. She read the third review:

Not a review so much as a question... I've been waiting for an announcement about the next installment of the series. Does anyone know if Robards is still writing or did she quit?

And there it was. All of Mae's fears mirrored back to her in a one, two, three, star punch. A punch to the gut that Mae had only herself to blame for as she knew exactly what was going to happen if she started reading reviews. The nice ones never stuck. The bad ones always felt more real as they clung to her feelings of inadequacy and amplified her own fears and doubts.

"Maybe they're right!" Mae exclaimed and abruptly pushed away from her desk. "Agh!" Scarpetta jumped to her feet, ready to rally, whatever the situation was. "Come on, let's go downstairs and help with dinner. I need to switch gears." The two headed out of the room where the now burned-out balsam candle couldn't even have covered the tension.

The kitchen, however, proved not to be a very good mood lightener either. Mae, trying to be productive in another facet of her life to make up for how bad she felt about her writing, had brought up their next steps for the ski center. As Mae had discussed with her parents before, it really did boil down to actual physical work time, and, of course, there were also less skiers coming but they'd deal with that issue after they handled the first one. They really needed another body out there on the trails because her parents couldn't work around the clock the way they used to. But hiring a full-time person meant more expenses and more time spent managing. It seemed that with Jack there to get them through the month, until Mae could spend more time outside, it would be ok. After which point, Mae would do a lot of the work and start brainstorming ideas to drum up a little extra business. They had gone over all of this before, but Mae had wanted to go through it again when she was feeling hypersensitive. Getting upset about something else was a wonderful way to distract herself from what she was originally upset about. The good news was that all the ski center's bills were paid through the New Year. And come January, if they needed to take a little time to restructure and reinvent, Mae could float them with the advance on her book.

"If you don't turn in the draft on the twenty-third, will they take your advance back?" asked her mom, wanting to figure out the lay of the land. Unfortunately, the lay of the land was an anxiety swamp for Mae. "Or, what if this Elizabeth Birk doesn't agree with your character, what happens then?"

"MOM!" Mae was out of bandwidth. "Why would you even put that out there? You know, maybe I won't finish! Maybe she'll hate it! Maybe I'm just not good enough and then you guys can go ahead and sell the ski center like you were going to do anyway." Mae switched from aggressively chopping red peppers to aggressively setting the table.

"Both your mother and I know that you're going to finish, Mae. What we don't want is for you to feel extra pressure because of us," her dad said, clearly trying to soothe the seas.

"I was trying to say, trying to get to, that we don't want you to do something with your book, like rush it or change it, because you feel responsible for everything here now," her mom added.

"That didn't seem like what you were trying to say," Mae felt stung. Maybe she shouldn't have brought up her fears about not finishing the book, or about Elizabeth Birk rejecting the draft, when she knew how vulnerable she was feeling. In fact, she absolutely knew she shouldn't have and so she tried to move on and shake it off. "I'm gonna go ask Jack if he wants to join us for dinner. Excuse me." She abruptly walked about of the kitchen and headed to the hall to grab her coat.

The cold air felt good on her face as Mae walked across the lot towards the ski center and around to the back. She could see the lights on in Jack's cabin as she approached. Mae walked up the steps and was about to knock on the door when she heard Jack talking on the other side. She quickly turned away, not wanting to interrupt him; she would just text him when she got back to the house. As she went to leave, the conversation inside floated through the door.

"I never visualized myself as being part of a family or a tight-knit group. I mean outside the Forest Service, and of course you and Rex, but otherwise, I just couldn't see it," Jack said, clearly talking to Mitzey. At Jack's words, Mae's face reddened as if she'd been slapped. She had known it. He was just a nice man, who she happened to have a lot in common with, who needed a job when she happened to have one. And that was it. He didn't want to be a part of something. She had been reading too far into his friendliness. She had made a fool of herself. Mae slunk off the steps and into the darkness taking the long way back to the house. Her mind raced. She felt silly, and dumb, and angry. She had her own stuff going on. If he didn't want to do family stuff with her, he should have just said so! By the time Mae got back to the house she was worked up to a full churn. She threw her jacket on the hall hook, kicked off her boots and beelined for the stairs.

"Is Jack coming in for dinner honey?" her mom's voice called.

"I don't know mom!" Mae again felt like a teenager.

"Well, did you…." Gloria pressed on with wanting the dinner details.

"He was on the phone," Mae interrupted. "I didn't want to bother him. You guys go ahead and eat. I need to write." She trudged up the stairs and into her room.

Mae stomped around in circles for a while before she wore herself out and sat back down at her desk. In the middle of her tantrum, she had an idea. Maybe the trick for her book was not make her character less flawed, but more flawed. Maybe she needed to add in a big whoopsie right in the middle of the story arc because she couldn't think of any more possible suspects to add for twists. Perhaps it was actually her main character, Laela, that had to go down a few dark roads. She opened up the laptop and scrolled back through the chapters to where she could start planting the seed.

Mae's emotions were intensely charged and she channeled it all into her writing. She stayed up all night, dragging Laela through a myriad of personal crisis in and around the actual mystery plot. Mae didn't even really know how her PI was going to come out at the other end at this point—she was way off the outline now. She lost all sense of time in her writing tunnel. The next day flew by with Mae only running downstairs to check and see if she was needed for anything, to walk and feed Scarpetta and to grab some food to take back upstairs. She'd been typing away for hours when Scarpetta pushed her nose through the door.

"Hey booboo," Mae said as she looked at her watch. "Oh, my word, I am so sorry! Did I miss dinner?" Scarpetta gave her a shrewd stare suggesting that Mae knew what she had done. With a repentant look Mae got up and headed to the kitchen. As she walked down the hall, she could hear her parents in the living room watching a movie. It sounded like *White Christmas*. Her dad had brought out the big holiday guns this evening, Mae thought as she opened the pantry and took out Scarpetta's food. She was filling the bowl when the phone rang. Mae grabbed the handset off the wall, taking a second to admire the classic beauty of the landline. In all the other rooms her parents had upgraded, but in the kitchen they still an old-fashioned type phone. It even had a curly cord. Every time Mae picked it, no matter what her mood, she had to giggle.

"Hello, Robards residence," Mae said into the timepiece.

"Mae?" A male voice questioned over the phone. "This is Derek Mumford."

"Oh, hi Derek! Yes, this is Mae. How was the family holiday party?" Mae spun the slinky-like chord around her fingers.

"It was good fun, thanks! Is Jack there by any chance?" Derek's question had the effect of turning Mae's ears hot.

"I think he's out in the cabin," she started to pace. "I can give you the number for out there? It's the same line as for the ski center."

"No, that's OK, I have it." He replied. "Did he happen to mention to you if he was considering the job offer?"

"What job offer?" Mae must have missed something.

"Oh…" Derek suddenly sounded uncomfortable. "We have an opening out at the huts in the notch. It would be perfect for Jack, if he was interested. I know he was looking, and those jobs are so few and far between right now." Derek started to speed up his cadence mid-explanation as if he had to sell Mae on it. "I was hoping to hear back today because I'd like to get him in there to meet everyone as soon as possible. I haven't been able to get him on his cell." He paused. "We, of course, would help you find someone else for the ski center. This way Jack could go back to working full-time with the Forest Service."

"Oh, of course…" Mae stammered. Her brain felt suddenly like it was too tight inside her head.

"OK, well, I'll try him out at the center. Thanks Mae."

"Yuh, no problem. Have a good night," Mae said as she hung up the phone and then stared at the wall. Mae immediately felt like Jack had been hiding this from her, a feeling she absolutely hated. She stood there rerunning the conversation through her mind. After a moment, Mae realized she was all wrapped up in the cord. She had started unwinding herself when she heard the door out in the hall open and a pair of heavy boots land on the entry way rug. Seconds later, Jack came around the corner beaming. He was all bundled up and had clearly been outside for a while in the cold night air. His face looked wind chapped. Sammy darted in behind him and skipped over to the stove to lay down next to Scarpetta. At least those two got to be close, Mae thought for a brief moment while she looked at the dogs enjoying the warmth together.

"I had the most beautiful walk on the back trails." Jack shared with Mae excitedly. "Those are some bewitching woods in the starlight!"

"Yeah, they sure are," Mae said while still trying to unwind herself.

"Lot going on there!" Jack said jovially as he saw that Mae was stuck in the phone cord. "I had an idea for…." He trailed off seemingly processing the look on Mae's face. "What's wrong?"

"Derek called. He wanted to know your answer about the job offer." Mae worked very hard to keep her tone regulated even though she felt angry at Jack for withholding information, and even angrier at herself, for enjoying when he was around.

"Oh. OK." Jack said totally neutral. "I'll call him back." The two then stood there awkwardly in the kitchen unsure of who should say what next. The silence stretched to the point where even the dogs seemed uncomfortable.

"We obviously wouldn't want to hold you back from a job," Mae decided she would start.

"No, of course not." Jack said seriously. "I wanted to make sure you guys…"

"Oh, well, we can handle it here," Mae interrupted a little more forcefully than she meant to. "We're not falling to pieces you know." She didn't want Jack to think she was incapable of handling it herself. She was mortified at the idea that he would somehow feel obligated, like she was some sort of charity case. She knew what a good heart he had after giving his job to Justin and didn't need him to not take a job for them.

"Of course, you can… And, of course, you're not," Jack hesitated. "Mae, I…"

"I mean it sounds like Derek is offering you a full-time job doing what you love. And I know that you don't like be *tied to a group* or whatever!" The words slipped out of Mae's mouth. She hadn't meant to repeat what she'd heard but her feelings were so raw she just plowed right through. "I really think you should take the job as soon as possible Jack. We appreciate everything you've done. We always get college kids home from school looking for some work this time of year, so we can piece it together until we can find someone permanent. Please don't worry about us."

"I've really enjoyed it here," Jack stammered. "And I am so grateful to you and your family... I did think the job sounded exciting so I..."

"So, great!" Mae interrupted again. She couldn't take it. She wanted to cry. And it made her so incredibly angry that she felt like her heart was breaking. This isn't about Jack, she told herself. These feelings were really because she had so much going on and she had hidden her anxiety away under dumb silly schoolgirl fantasies for Jack instead of dealing with all the real adult things she needed to be dealing with. This is work for him, she reminded herself. And you Mae, she yelled inside her own head, have your own work to be doing. She clapped her hands together. "Well! This seems to all have happened for the best then." She started walking back towards the stairs. "Thank you, Jack. It's been very nice.

I am really happy this led to you finding a new place. Derek said he was hoping you could get up there right away to meet everyone. Feel free to leave all your stuff in the cabin for as long as you want." And with that Mae turned and headed upstairs, leaving Jack standing in the kitchen, speechless.

The Holiday Breakdown

Chapter 15 - Finally, A Cookie Baking Montage!

*M*ae sat in her room until everyone had gone to bed and the house was totally quiet. The days had flown by so fast that she hadn't even realized it was already the night of the twentieth. Three days until her draft was due and five days until Christmas. She normally loved the holiday season so much, but except for a few moments, most of which had been with Jack, she realized that sadly she hadn't had much time to celebrate or prepare at all. Mae reminded herself that there was no time like the present and crept downstairs. Once in the kitchen she began to search through all the drawers until she found her favorite cookie cutters. A little rummaging through the fridge and pantry and all the items she needed were laid out on the kitchen counter. Outside watching *Lord of the Rings,* nothing quite soothed Mae's soul like late night treats. She mixed together the ingredients for the dough and started rolling it out. Using the task at hand as sort of a meditative device, as all of the events of the last few days came crashing through her mind. Mae very much wanted Jack to have a job he loved, but she also felt like she should have been told right away. This not being told immediately upset her deeply. She didn't want anyone worrying that she couldn't handle the news. But, at the same time, they really did need someone to cover the work, especially now when she was so tight on her deadline, and it hurt her to think that Jack hadn't thought to give them a heads up. Quite frankly, it just didn't seem like him at all and that made Mae even more irritated for judging him so incorrectly. Had his plan been to wait to tell them until he'd made up his mind completely, been hired already and was on his way? She rolled the dough harder and harder until it was almost as thin as a tissue.

"Dang it!" Mae exclaimed so upset at herself for being in this position. She ripped off a piece of the dough to give it a taste. It was delicious! Before Mae realized what had happened, half of the flour from the rolling pin had managed to find its way onto her face and about a quarter of the raw dough had found its way into her mouth.

"In the baking scenes in movies they usually cook them first," Kurt Robards said warmly. Mae turned around quickly with a little jump—she had not heard him come downstairs.

"And everyone just eats one perfect cookie. Never the whole batch. Who has that kind of willpower?!" Mae asked earnestly with flour all over her face.

"It's absolutely ridiculous," her father agreed.

"Ridiculous!" Mae emphasized, and then she started grinning, overcome by the absurdity of the entire situation. Kurt Robards looked at his daughter who was covered in flour and burst out into laughter. The two fed off each other's amusement and fell into a fit of gulps and tears. It felt good to laugh, Mae thought as she started rolling the dough out again, covering up all the places where she had left fingerprints. Her father grabbed a few of the cookie cutters and got to work as well. The two were almost done with cutting out the shapes and placing them onto the pan before anyone spoke again.

"Did you talk to Jack about the job offer?" Her dad asked.

"What?" Mae was shocked. "How did you know about it? Did everyone know but me?" She felt stung all over again. How long had everyone known? Were they hiding it from her because they all thought she was so gaga over him that she couldn't take hearing simple facts? She stuffed a whole raw cookie into her mouth, willing it into reality that salmonella was not a thing.

"Mae," her father said, clearly recognizing the unwillingness to wait for the cookies to be baked as a sign of a rising emotional tide. "Derek called Jack earlier this afternoon. You were inside writing all day and it seemed like you were on such a roll that no one wanted to interrupt you. Plus, Jack was waiting to hear back about some more details of the job. It was unclear when they wanted to meet him and when it started. We had been discussing what the alternatives were for us as far as finding someone else depending on when he would need to leave. I'm sure he told you all that?" Mae said nothing in response, her face reddening. "Mae?" her father looked at her gently.

"I think maybe I didn't really give him time to explain himself. I, for some reason, thought he had known since we saw Derek the other day at Renee's and that he didn't tell me right away because he either felt bad for me because I was in over my head, or he felt like he was obligated to be here, which I didn't want either." Mae grabbed a handful of red sprinkles and mashed them onto a Santa cut out.

"Of course, we want him to take the job, honey," her father said as he added some chocolate chip buttons to a snowman cookie.

"Well, of course! I want him to take the job, too!" Mae said passionately. And she firmly meant it. It would be so great if Jack could be back doing what he loved full-time. She just felt like she was somehow the butt of a joke, or like everyone was feeling sorry for her. Hurt by the words she had heard Jack say over the phone in his cabin to Mitzey, she assumed he was wishing he could just let her down easy.

"Here's what I think," Kurt started. "Can I tell you what I think?" Mae nodded. "I think you probably got so upset thinking that he was feeling sorry for you, your words, whatever that means. And, because you are a person who so values people being able to do what they love, that you, maybe, bulldozed the situation by not giving him a moment to say what he was thinking because you felt so defensive around it. And who could blame you, Mae! It's been a very overwhelming month with a lot of changes. You have a lot happening."

"I don't know," Mae said. But she totally knew, her dad was right. So, after a brief moment, she acquiesced. "Bulldoze? Dad. Come on?!"

"I could be wrong," her dad smiled and shrugged.

"I wonder where I get it from," Mae's eyes drifted to the direction of her parent's room.

"Two of the most headstrong ladies in the game! God bless us." Kurt Robards smiled.

"I'm sorry if I've been short tempered the past two days dad. I just felt like I made a mess of everything," Mae confided.

"What is this making a mess of everything nonsense?" Kurt put his arm around his daughter. "Mae, if we haven't made it clear, we are so happy you wanted to come home and keep the ski center open with us."

"You're sure?" Mae asked genuinely because she couldn't tell anymore.

"Very!" her dad stated firmly. "Both your mom and I are. And we know you'll figure out your book. Mae you've had writing in your heart ever since you were a little girl. You'll get through this hump. I believe in you." Mae's eyes suddenly felt like they were swollen. It was so good to hear these words. Her father continued, "We can make this place work with or without the advance from your book if you want to tell that lady to…to stuff it!" At this Mae started to laugh again. Her father never suggested that someone should *stuff it!*

Those were some fighting words for Kurt Robards. It was such an incredible relief to hear. They had said it before in passing but Mae hadn't really taken it in or even realized just how incredibly responsible for everything she'd felt until the weight started to lift from her shoulders.

"Thanks dad," Mae said gratefully.

"And for Pete's sake, Mae!" her dad said. It was another rarely heard phrase conveyed such passion that it caused Mae to giggle again. "Just be honest with the man! And give him a second to say what he wants as well, and then just go from there." He wiped some flour off Mae's face.

"OK dad."

"And let me have some of that." Kurt tried a piece of the raw dough. "You know, it really is so much better this way!"

"RIGHT?! I mean for Pete's sake!" Mae laughed again, repeating her dad's words. They were just two peas in a possible food poisoning pod, she thought before stealing one more very tiny piece of the yummy raw dough.

The Holiday Breakdown

Chapter 16 - Who's Rosemary Clooney Now

The next morning, Mae was out in the woods with Scarpetta looking for a small tree to put in her room. Feeling like she'd missed out on much of the joy of the season, Mae had decided that what she obviously needed was a little tree decorating to lighten the mood. That would make everything feel better, or at least she hoped it would. Mae had always loved exploring their back woods off the trails. She wandered through the morning light in search of the perfect tree. The cold air felt refreshing and helped clear her head. Jack had left at dawn. Now that Mae knew Jack and her parents had in fact discussed the whole job situation, and that the only reason she hadn't heard earlier was because they all didn't want to interrupt her writing, she felt dumb and wanted to apologize. She shouldn't have assumed. He was being responsible, and, of course, had gone over everything with her parents before heading out. Mae's dad had said that he and Mae's mom could cover everything while Jack went up to the notch for a few days to see if it was a good fit, and upon Jack's return, when they knew all the details, they would figure the rest out. Even with understanding how the job offer had unfolded, it didn't make Mae feel any better about the conversation that she had overheard outside the cabin between Jack and Mitzey.

Mae knew though that she needed to take responsibility and make amends. She decided that she would tell Jack how sorry she was when he got back. If he could accept her apology then they would be friends, but it was never going to be any more than that. Which was fine, she told herself. Plus, she was so close to her draft deadline, just two days left, and she needed her primary focus to remain there. She had gone back in and added more personal conflict for her main character. In Mae's first four books the biggest conflicts were with the other characters and, of course, in the mystery itself. Obviously, Laela had gone through personal changes in each book, but the major battles where outside of her. With this book, Mae had added a much larger internal battle as well. She was almost to the end and through the character's new transformation it had left her at an interesting crossroads. She could, in fact, have Laela change into this new woman, a detective who was more in line with what Birk was hoping for—a classic, stable, more structured detective. Or, Mae could double down and have the new changes lead the character to be even more imprudent and fanciful, and then if Birk didn't like it they could always go to another publisher. Mae's thoughts travelled down both avenues, weighing the pros and cons, again and again until she was interrupted by the sound of her phone ringing. Mae looked at the number and after a slight hesitation she picked up.

"Well, hello there Mitzey!" Mae exclaimed, both excited to hear from her new friend but also embarrassed that Mitzey must already know that Jack and her weren't going to work out.

"Mae! So great to hear your voice!" Mitzey's warmth emanated from the phone.

"Have you seen Rex lately?" Mae teased, wanting to skip the feelings of vulnerability.

"What?!" Mitzey became all of a sudden very flustered. "Um. Well. Of course, he lives across the street. Which you know and… MAE, that's not why I called. I wanted to check in on you and Jack," Mitzey said grabbing the reins of the conversation and turning it back on Mae.

"Oh. Well, I'm sure you've heard. He's taking a job up at the notch," Mae stated this with an upbeat and kind tone to cover up that what she felt was just a whole lot of sad. Not because of the job at all, she was genuinely happy for him, but because Mae had to face the fact that she had really hoped there was something more between them and how much she'd enjoyed having him around. Foolish, she reminded herself and shook her head as if trying to physically dispel the feelings.

"What?" Mitzey asked.

"A job at the notch!" Mae repeated loudly into the phone in case they had a bad connection.

"No, I heard you. I just, well, that wasn't what I was expecting you to say," Mitzey admitted.

"Oh?" Mae was slightly shocked.

"I talked to him the other night," Mitzey continued.

"Yeah, I know." The words slipped out before Mae had consciously given then permission to leave her mouth.

"Oh, did he tell you?" Mitzey sounded all of a sudden oddly pleased.

"Not exactly," Mae said as she took a deep breath. She was just going to have to admit to the whole thing and hated herself already for the words that were about to come out of her mouth. "I was about to knock on his door, I was coming to invite him to eat with us!" Mae explained in a way that she hoped sounded unlike a person who would intentionally eavesdrop. "And as I came up the steps to his cabin, I accidentally overheard him talking to you. I really didn't mean to hear it, Mitzey. I felt like I'd invaded a personal conversation."

"And what do you hear?" Mitzey pressed.

"I heard him say that besides you and Rex and the Forest Service he just didn't see himself as the kind of person who would be a part of a family. Or to function as group, or whatever." Mae reddened at the memory. She was so embarrassed.

"And?" Mitzey pressed again.

"And what?" Mae said slightly exasperated. "That's it! He doesn't want to be part of...of a thing..." Mae stumbled on the right words. "And, I get it. I understand. It's a lot. ANYWAYS. I didn't want to be any more of a bother, clearly, I'd been a bother already. He was here for a job and maybe I was hoping for more. Even though I'd never said that to him! But, somehow, he saw that, and didn't want any part of it. So, that was that. I went back to the house to leave him be."

"Ohhhhhhhhh.... Ms. Mae," Mitzey said as if coming to some kind of an understanding. "You missed the second part of the conversion. *Until now,* is what Jack told me. He hadn't felt that way *until now.* Then he went on to say some VERY nice things about you, and about your family, which I won't repeat because they are for him to tell you."

"What? Really?" Mae had stopped walking earlier in the conversation but at this realization she leaned against a tree to stabilize herself, getting sap all over her jacket in the process.

"What we have here is a classic *White Christmas* mix up. In the movie, Rosemary Clooney's character overhears a phone call, but she only hears the first part so she thinks that…"

"I'm very familiar with *White Christmas* Mitzey. In fact, I'm pretty sure I even used it as example for you and Rex." Mae was going to bring up that relationship as many times as she possibly could to move the attention away from herself.

"Well, that's what happened here!" Mitzey exclaimed, undeterred. "So, I guess when he got offered another job you pushed him right out the door thinking that he was only there because he felt obligated in some way."

"I felt embarrassed. I was worried that I was making a fool out of myself," Mae admitted. "You know for a woman who can't see that her lovely neighbor has the hots for her you sure are pretty good at reading a situation."

"He doesn't have the hots for me…or whatever you called it!" Mitzey protested.

"Yes, he does! Ohhhhhhh Mitzey, what are we going to do?" Mae stood up straight and tried to wipe the sap from her jacket. It was no use, she was going to have to get some rubbing alcohol involved. She sighed inwardly about her inability to keep anything clean and started wiggling her feet hoping to warm them up after standing in the same place.

"I think these things have a way of working themselves out. They did in *White Christmas!*" Mitzey was staying strong with the reference. "Remember when…"

"Mitzey!" Mae blurted out as her feet began to feel like they had blood running through them again. "Are you kidding me? I'm not gonna open the barn doors and all of a sudden it starts snowing while Jack and I kiss behind a tree." Just the reference to herself and Jack kissing made all the blood rush out of Mae's feet and run somewhere else entirely. She suddenly felt disoriented and leaned back on the same tree, totally re-sapping. "Are you kidding me?!" Mae exclaimed again.

"We'll see," said Mitzey with a knowing tone. Then, "Mae, so sorry, I have to go. I have people coming through the door to check in."

"Alright, thanks for calling Mitzey. Go get your Danny Kaye!" Mae said trying to get the last one in. Mitzey ignored her comment and wished Mae well before ringing off.

Mae continued to stand in the cold snow and stare off into the woods. Scarpetta had been playing in the trees, following new scents and sounds. Mae slowly walked over to where the pooch had seemed to find something particularly interesting to paw at.

"I had it completely wrong," Mae said to Scarpetta. "And, I totally overreacted!" Scarpetta looked back at her with caring eyes, then she tilted her head and raised her jowls in a way that seemed to suggest to Mae that Scarpetta thought that this wasn't the first time. "Ugh! You're right. OK! Let's find this tree, get back to the house, finish this book, and then we'll figure out how to apologize. I hope there's still time…" Mae stopped herself before finishing the sentence. She couldn't believe she had been about to say *I hope there's still time to save Christmas.* She was NOT a woman in a Christmas romance she reminded herself.

Chapter 17 - A Change in Perspective

*M*ae was back in her room. She and Scarpetta had found a perfect little tree on the return walk to the house and it was now set up in the corner. Mae had out a box of ornaments that she'd brought back from LA (which she had brought from New York after having originally brought them from New Hampshire to begin with). They were all the homemade decorations from when Mae was a kid and were among her most prized possessions. She pulled out one of the treasures. It was half a pinecone covered in sparkles with a picture of her from grade school. She recalled that they'd made them in class as gifts for their parents, but somehow Mae had managed to end up with it. She looked at the photo of her younger self. Goofy. Too tall. A big ole head. Smiling wildly. Probably totally thinking about some fantasy world. Since Mae could remember she had always been lost in her imagination. It was a quality that she actually appreciated about herself. It did of course also lead to the problem of overthinking, but that was the darker side of what she felt was the gift she had been given. When she was young her imagination hadn't held with it the second guessing, the living out all of the horrible scenarios, it was just a place where Mae pretended to be a detective, or a wizard, or as Reverend Woods had pointed out, a wizard detective. Looking at the fading photo Mae believed that young Mae, the Mae in the photo, would think that what she was doing now was pretty cool. Creating stories for a living, with a rowdy and unusual heroine who didn't follow the rules, who wasn't embarrassed for being different, and perhaps even a little goofy too. Mae hung the ornament on the tree. I'm not going to let you down now, Mae thought as she stood and walked over to her computer.

Mae opened her laptop and started an email:

Dear Neal,

I hope this note finds you all in cheerful construction paper Santa hats. After our last conversation I've been doing some deep thinking. I appreciate that you said you would back whatever decision I made. I've come to the conclusion that I must remain true to the character as I see her. But do not fret! I am moments away from being finished and will have the draft to you by the morning of the 23rd. And that's a Christmas promise! (And yes, I know that's the day after tomorrow.) Also, please pass on to Birk that I'm a woodswoman now.

Gumdrops & Sugarplum Faeries,
Mae

Mae took a deep breath and pressed send. The computer made a whooshing sound as the letter flew out of her hands and towards Neal. It was done.

"So, there's that!" Mae said more steadily than she felt as she looked over at her dog. Scarpetta came over and sat on Mae's feet, looking up at her with eyes that screamed, *FINALLY!* Mae laughed at the expression on Scarpetta's face and got back to writing. Now that she had made the decision, it was time to close it out.

On the opposite coast, Neal Michaels was seated at his desk in his home office. He heard Mae's email come in and immediately opened it. Upon reading the message he broke into a wide smile. Then Neal opened up a message of his own to send:

Dear Ms. Birk,

> *Mae and I have discussed all your notes regarding her main character and, of course, appreciate you taking the time and vested interest in the series. Upon much contemplation, Mae has decided to remain true to the voice of Laela Sarno and to the audience who have been dedicated readers of the series. We will, of course, have the draft to you by the deadline of December 23rd, as was promised. At such time you can decide whether or not you want to continue our relationship. Mae has requested that I pass on her warmest holiday wishes from New Hampshire where she has decided to live with her family.*
>
> *Best,*
> *Neal Michaels*

Neal smiled as he sent the message off to Birk. Good for you Mae, he thought. He then rose from his desk and headed back into the living room to see if there were any more Santa hats that needed to be made.

On the other side of Los Angeles, Elizabeth Birk was scrolling through the emails on her phone when the message from Neal came in. She opened it immediately, interested in seeing what he had to say. As she scanned the note, she was momentarily overcome with what could only be described as mild shock.

"Holiday wishes indeed...well, I never!" She exclaimed to her office walls just as Steven peaked his head in through the door.

"Sorry?" Steven asked, assuming the exclamation had been directed at him.

"I've just had a message from Mae Robards' agent," Birk explained. "She won't be making the changes I suggested. That I strongly suggested, I might add. Well, we'll have to do something about that!" Steven said nothing in reply to this. He, in fact, quite liked the Robards' series as it was but wasn't about to mention that at this moment. "Is there something you wanted to ask?" Birk questioned, still full of a global irritation.

"Oh, yes," Steven responded, reminded of why he had come down to her office in the first place. "There's a message from your daughter on line one. She said she's going to be able to make it home after all. I saved the message so you can listen to all the details."

"Clare? Coming home?" For a brief moment it appeared that Elizabeth Birk was shaken. "I thought she wasn't coming. I was going to skip Christmas this year. I… I don't have anything ready," she said in a voice that one could say was borderline exposed.

"No, no we don't, do we? Maybe it's time we get a little Christmas spirit going on in here then." Steven smiled broadly at his boss, who he knew from hearing missed messages and seeing snippets of emails, had a rift with her daughter and had just not been that same since they'd stopped talking. "I was going to get a tree this afternoon. Would you like to come?" It was time to turn this holiday season around.

Chapter 18 - What is This? A Chick Flick?!

The next day Mae was still at her desk typing away. The tree was now all set up and twinkling in the corner of her room. She had taken a few breaks to eat and to walk around outside circling the house with Scarpetta; stretching all of their legs and trying to get some fresh air into her brain. Mae was on a roll and in the final throws of closing out the book. She had texted her friends to let them know what her response to Elizabeth Birk had been. They all had responded with supportive words and celebratory emojis. It felt good. She was about to stand up and stretch her legs again when there was a knock on the door. So lost in her writing, Mae hadn't even heard anyone coming up the steps.

"Hello?" Mae said as she got up and headed across the room.

"Hey Mae!" It was Renee's voice.

"Come in! Come in!" Mae was so excited to see her friend that she tripped over one of the many things she'd thrown on the floor and just as Renee was opening the door Mae fell directly into her. They both gasped and then started laughing. Mae was a constant hazard.

"I brought these for you," Renee said after the two friends had righted themselves. She held out a bag of what looked, and smelled, like baked goods. "More fresh crullers to say congrats on your decision with your editor, I know that was big! Tim made them again. I was going to leave them downstairs, but your mom thought you might want a quick snack break."

"Oh, this is wonderful. Thank you, Renee!" Mae was delighted. She reached into the bag, pulled out one of the chocolatey treasures, and took a bite. "SO GOOD!" She exclaimed.

"I swung by the office thinking I would say hello to Jack, but your mom said he wasn't here. And then she gave me A LOOK. Anything you want to tell me?" Renee sat down and crossed her legs in a move which suggested that Mae should spill it.

"Ughhhhhhhh, Renee!" Mae groaned. "I made a big whoopsie. I overheard Jack say—NOT ON PURPOSE MIND YOU—I was going over to the cabin to see if he wanted to eat dinner and as I was walking up the steps...never mind, those details are irrelevant." Mae regrouped so she could summarize, skipping over the accidental eavesdropping section. "I wrongly thought that Jack had confided in Mitzey, the woman I told you about who owns the motel, that he didn't want to be here, or that maybe I wanted him to be a part of something he wasn't ready to be a part of. I don't know what I thought exactly, but it turns out that he had said the exact opposite. Apparently, he told Mitzey, who I spoke to yesterday, that he actually loved being here and being a part of things. But this was already after I'd found out he'd been offered a job! Which was another misunderstanding that I thought he was hiding from me, for a myriad of horrible reasons that I also made up in my head. So, I pushed him out the door because, of course, I want him to take it the job. We all want him to take it. But I also didn't want to hear what he had to say because I had in my head that he felt sorry for me for wanting him here when he didn't want to be. Anyways! That's it." Mae took a deep breath from her run-on explanation.

"You never let him say what he was thinking at all?" Renee asked like it was a question, but they both knew she was really making a statement.

"No," Mae said, breaking off another piece of cruller. "I did not."

"Good to see some things don't change. You always hated feeling vulnerable, Mae!" Renee grabbed a cruller out of the bag as well.

"Honestly, I'm embarrassed that we're even having this conversation. I don't like feeling vulnerable?! What is this a Lifetime movie? I'm literally turning into a trope. I want to throw up!" Mae dramatically hurled herself onto her bed.

"Cut the crap Mae, you know I'm right," Renee grinned. "Also, you love Lifetime! Don't think you're fooling me one little bit." She pulled off a piece of her cruller and playfully threw it at her friend. It hit Mae right smack-dab in forehead, and, of course, she then promptly ate the errant chunk as it would have been a travesty to waste it. Across the room Mae's phone started ringing on her desk. She pulled herself up to her feet to go look at it.

"Oh, it's a FaceTime from my friend Julie in LA!" Mae explained to Renee.

"Pick it up!" Renee said, gesturing with her hands.

"Julie! Hi!" Mae said. "I'm here with Renee. I've told both of you about each other." Mae turned the phone around so Julie and Renee could see one another in the

FaceTime. They both waved and then she flipped the phone back.

"I was just rereading your email about the editor and was so pumped for you that I wanted to call!" Julie said, clearly very happy that Mae had gotten over this emotional hump.

"Thank you so much, Jules. I gotta tell ya, it does feel really good. And, if I need a new publisher then that's what has to happen."

"That's right!" Julie cheered for her friend. "Is Renee over because you two are celebrating or because you banished Jack already? I noticed that you didn't say anything about him in the email."

"What? Julie! Banished? Why would you say that?" Mae looked at her friend like she had no idea what she was talking about.

"That's totally what's happening!" Renee yelled from across the room.

"Oh, you!" Mae scolded as she walked over to sit next to Renee so they could both talk into the phone.

"Feels like a scene from something, doesn't it?" Julie smiled at both women through the screen. "Your friends stepping in to tell you to let your guard down and to have faith in things. Especially in yourself!"

"I was JUST saying that! And it feels quite gross to be honest." Mae over rolled her eyes and then stole another bite of Renee's cruller.

"Get over it!" Julie laughed. "And THAT looks delicious. WOW."

"It is!" Mae exclaimed. "Renee made them! She owns a bakery, I think I mentioned it to you previously, and the gym! Oh, and they are so good."

"My son made this batch actually," Renee said with pride. "He's becoming quite the gifted baker. I can get your address from Mae and send you some if you like?"

"I would love that. Thanks so much! So, I assume you guys were already deep in the boy sitch?" Julie was now speaking directly to Renee, bypassing Mae entirely.

"We are working on it," Renee explained ardently. "Mae is going to have to apologize and allow herself to be vulnerable."

"Oh, this will be good!" Julie jumped on board.

"OK! OK! OK!" Mae said, waving her hands at her friends as if they were having way too much fun with the situation. "This is the worst conversation I've ever been in!" Mae dramatically joked. Now it was Julie and Renee's turn to roll their eyes.

"You know what I like," Julie changed the tone of the conversation. "I like that you and Jack have such different careers, as far as what you do. But, they are similar in that you're occupied for long stretches of time. I was thinking about that when you told me about Jack's trip to Alaska where he met that guy that your family knows. It would be nice for you to date someone who understands a job that takes a person out for a while. Sarah and I have that, and it's meant all the world to me."

"What is going on over there?" Sarah called from somewhere behind Julie and then stuck her head into the screen. "I heard you over here being complimentary." She gave her wife's head a love rub.

"Renee, this is Sarah. Sarah, this is Renee. I'm sure you've both heard me dropping crazy compliments about one another." Mae smiled as the two women waved at each other. "You know Jules, on the drive back from Kentucky, Jack and I actually discussed just that. What you said, about how hard it was to date because no one understood our schedules."

"Did you now?! That's something! How come I didn't hear about this?!" Julie prodded.

"I mean, because it was just a conversation and maybe it didn't necessarily mean anything except that we both have erratic schedules. Also! Maybe I scared him away entirely, so what does it matter anyway? I don't want to get my hopes up." Mae protested.

"Come on, Mae, get your hopes up!" It sounded to Mae like Renee was all of a sudden doing a character, but she just couldn't figure out who it was.

"What's the worst that could happen?" Sarah joined in.

"I mean…" Mae picked out what she thought was clearly the worst of the options. "He doesn't feel the same, and I feel stupid."

"Mae, that is the risk of romance!" Renee enthused, very heavy on the word *romance*. She was shaking her shoulders and Mae was now sure she was speaking with an accent.

"Oh! I got it." Mae pointed to Renee. "Are you being the candlestick guy from *Beauty & The Beast*?"

"Lumière!" Sarah jumped on it.

"Yes! Lumière!" Mae clapped at Sarah for getting it.

"I am French yes, speaking zee language of luv." Renee was going hard. "But pas moi, I am not zis candlestick" All the women laughed.

"Well," Julie said, and Mae recognized the tone from her friend, she about to change the subject again. "What is happening with the draft?"

"It is due tomorrow! I just have to wrap it up," Mae said excitedly. "I was so stuck, as you all know. I kept feeling like something was wrong or missing. I tried to add more twists and turns going on around Laela, but then I realized I needed to add them going on inside of her."

"That is verrrrrrryyyyyyyyy interesting." Julie said not so subtly.

"Yes," Renee agreed. "What an odd coincidence!" Renee wiggled her brows and pronounced it *donce,* as she was clearly still in character.

"You really love being the candlestick guy, don't you?!" Mae goaded.

"Shedding light on all I see!" Renee laughed again.

"I was just going into the last chunk," Mae continued, smiling. "I went back and re-read and re-edited, which usually I don't do until I'm entirely finished. But I wanted to feel the lead up again and fix anything egregious so I could just focus on the finale!" Mae was definitely excited.

"Oh, going into the last bit, it does feel very prophetic!" Sarah added.

"Are you guys about to get all crystals and moons and stuff on me here?" Mae joked as she pretended to be appalled, but deep down she loved it.

"Where did you leave off? Can we have a taste?" Renee asked. And then added, "Ugh, sorry! That's probably not appropriate to ask. I can wait until the book comes out!"

"No, it's fine." Normally Mae didn't share any of her writing with friends while it was still in the draft stages, but this felt like something new. Mae grabbed her laptop. She scrolled to the last paragraph that she had written and handed it to Renee.

"I don't much buy into the phrase *the road to hell is paved with good intentions...*" Renee started reading Mae's words out loud, which sort of made Mae cringe but much less than expected. These were her friends, her support team, and it actually felt kind of nice to share. Renee continued, "I think that's just something people who lack good intentions tell themselves, and consequently others, so they don't have to feel guilty about never having had them to begin with. Of course, people with genuinely good intentions do sometimes get caught up in something that they didn't want to happen. Like a Netflix binge, when you only meant to watch one episode. Then, seemingly all of a sudden, it's days later, you're still watching, you haven't showered and you're eating condiments. But, having good intentions means you reassess a situation. I, however, was forced to a point of reassessment a little before I would have reached it on my own by a loud knock on the door. *Leala Sarno? Please open up.* And it was time for me to face my actions, head on, with no makeup and not having shaved my legs past mid-calf in weeks."

"Head on!" Sarah repeated. "I love it!"

"Yay, thanks for sharing with us!" Renee said, seemingly delighted.

"Thank YOU," Mae said to her friends. "You guys don't think it too *silly and meandering?*" Mae asked, bringing out the air quotes again in a quick moment of self-conscious, self-doubt.

"Silly and meandering," Julie repeated. "Mae, were you reading reviews again? Oh, my word! I thought we weren't doing that anymore, you know better!"

"Yeah, you know what they say…" added Sarah.

"What do they say?" Mae always loved Sarah's positive view of the world quote selections.

233

"You could be the sweetest peach in the entire orchard, and there will still be someone who doesn't like peaches," Sarah recited cheerfully.

"Mae!" Julie warmed. "Yes, you have a fun first person story telling voice. Who cares if some people think it's too, whatever. So, what! It's your voice and that's what's so great about it. You know this! That's why you sent that message to the editor doubling down, betting on yourself. It's time to throw it all away Mae, the self-doubt, the questioning. Be free of it. Enjoy your writing again!"

"Thank you, Jules!" Mae felt like she was being given a Rocky montage type speech for Christmas. She felt so lucky.

"Renee, might I say that you have the most incredible reading voice. You could do voiceovers if you were ever interested," Julie added.

"Thank you!" Renee glowed.

"Julie is a director!" Mae reminded Renee as she beamed at all her talented friends. "Renee is in the church choir," she informed Julie. "And was always the lead in all of our school plays!"

"Oh, my goodness, I think I've just had an idea!" Sarah jumped in excitedly. "Remember when you said that you'd like to self-produce your own audiobooks? What if you guys did a little *Finding Laela* audio series! Julie directs. I'll edit. Renee reads."

"I love it!" Julie and Renee clapped in unison and then everyone looked at Mae.

"Of course, you may have changed your mind," Julie said gently.

"And you may have already thought of a specific actor you wanted, if you ever decided to do one." Renee added.

"It's just a thing that popped out of my mouth," Sarah said. "I know you have a lot happening." Mae could tell her friends were rushing in, in case she suddenly felt cornered.

"No! I LOVE this idea!" And she did. "It's so good Sarah! I mean, if everyone was up for it! I could add padding to one of the rooms in the ski center, like a little sound booth. Julie and Sarah, you could Zoom in."

"This is so great!" Julie exclaimed. "Do remember when I first tried to get you to start listening to audiobooks?" She asked Mae and then broke out into a fit of laughter.

"Tell me!" Renee piped in. "I want to know what ridiculous thing Mae said. I can tell it's a good one already."

"Renee!" Mae feigned shock. "You guys are acting like I say crazy stuff!"

"Imagine!" Julie laughed.

"Well, tell us then," Sarah prodded.

"I just..." Mae started, knowing that it was indeed a ridiculous thing she had said, especially coupled with the passion she had originally said it with. "OK, so Jules was trying to get me to listen to this series on audiobook and I, I was appalled. I didn't like the way people presented audiobooks. They'd be telling you about something they were reading, as if they were reading it themselves and then you would find out that they were being read to. I mean, it's more like I don't agree with the terminology. It's just so incredibly misleading."

"I love this so much. Tell them exactly what you said to me Mae," Julie pushed, still laughing.

"I think what I said was something to the extent of, *Oh I can read my own words, thank you. I've worked hard to be able to follow along myself!*" Mae remembered being a real prig about it. But then Julie had gotten her to actually listen to one and it was so incredible. The man reading the book had woven in and out of the different characters—Mae had gotten completely lost in the magic. It was genuinely wonderful. "Then I listened to one, just to make Jules happy, of course..."

"Which I deeply appreciate," Julie added. "And then she said..."

"And then," Mae took up the sentence. "Well, I tried to switch back to reading the series myself and I was sitting with Julie at the park and I..."

"She put down the book, looked at me and totally seriously said, *What I gotta read my own words now? This is terrible. It's how the pilgrims must have felt wagon wheeling across America. There must be a better way!*" Julie broke out into full laughter. "I will never forget. It was so funny to me. You were so serious."

"Thank goodness a girl can change her mind!" Mae said, and then started laughing as well. She looked at her three friends, she felt so extremely loved and so incredibly grateful. "Thank you. You really are the best friends a girl could ever dream of."

The Holiday Breakdown

Chapter 19 - At Dawn from the East

*M*ae had been in a much better mood after the conversation with her friends. She felt excited about future possibilities; something she realized she hadn't felt in a very long, long time. Not just since she had decided to come back to New Hampshire, but stretching back months and months prior. It was so good to feel eager again, like she was looking forward to things with confidence.

Mae's new enthusiasm had carried her through the rest of the day and most of the night. She had only taken writing breaks to check on Scarpetta and her parents and to grab dinner. Sometime after midnight Mae had passed out on her bed for a quick nap but had woken up soon thereafter and gotten right back at it. Now, it was just before dawn and Mae was seated at her computer typing the very last words of her fifth book. What a glorious feeling!

"We did it!" Mae excitedly whispered down to Scarpetta, who had had been laying at her feet for the past few hours. Just then she heard a quiet knock. Mae got up and gently opened the door. Her mom stood there in her bathrobe, hot mugs of coffee in each hand.

"Honey," her mom whispered. "I heard you typing away when I got up to get a midnight snack, and again when I woke up to stoke the fires this morning."

"Yeah, I was up most of the night," Mae said as she opened the door all way. "Come in, come in!"

"I brought you some coffee!" Her mother handed her a cup of the steaming goodness and Mae immediately took a grateful sip.

"So delicious. Thank you, mom!" She took a moment to bask in the thrill of the coffee. "Here, come sit down." Mae led the way back across the room to her desk. The two women sat in silence for a brief moment in the quiet early morning.

"I'm so glad you're here honey. I'm really proud of you!" Her mom looked at her with caring eyes.

"Really?" Mae felt almost at a loss for words at the tender moment.

"Of course, Mae. More than anything!" Gloria Robards got up and kissed Mae on the head. The sweet gesture filled Mae's heart. It meant so much to her to hear those words.

"Thank you, mom," Mae said from the very bottom of her soul.

"I'll leave you to it then," Gloria said as she stood up and turned as if she was about to head back to the door. "I didn't want to interrupt your writing, I just wanted to bring you some coffee. I know today is the big day!"

"Mom!" Mae glowed. "I finished. I finished! Right before you came in actually… I was just typing the last line. Can you imagine? I did it!"

"Oh, wow! Yes honey, I can imagine!" Her mother sat back down, almost breathless. "Congratulations Mae!" The two women clinked their mugs in celebration. Rays of pink and orange light started to tumble in through the window. Mae's room was on the side of the house facing east, and on the occasions where she was up (as she had hardly ever gotten up that early—it was way more likely that she had stayed up all night), Mae loved to watch the dawn enter her room. It always reminded her of her favorite scene from *Lord of the Rings,* when it felt like the battle had been lost and Gimli says, *Look the sun is rising.* They had made it through the darkest night. Mae blushed slightly as she remembered that that was also part of Jack's favorite scene as well.

"Anyways!" Mae slapped her leg, bringing herself back to the moment.

"It's ANYWAY, honey," her mother corrected. Mae was about to give her mom a good groan but then she burst out into laughter. What a couple of wild cards they were, Mae thought as reached out to hug her mom, and thank goodness for that!

A few hours later Mae was showered, dressed, and sitting at the kitchen counter staring at her phone having another cup of coffee. She dialed Neal and listened as it went straight into his voicemail. She looked over at the clock on the wall and cringed thinking about how early it was in Los Angeles.

"Hey! Hey! Hey! Neal, it's me. Mae Robards, ughh, you know who it is. Gahhh! Now I sound like my mom...anyways. AnyWAY! I realized, at this moment, that it's extremely early there. My apologies! BUT I have good news. Great news, actually! Neal! I finished! I'm sending the draft to you now! And happy day before Christmas Eve!" Mae hung up the phone and popped open her laptop. She addressed a message to Neal and attached the draft of the finished book.

Neal-

Here she is!

-Mae

With a thrilling whoosh, Mae pressed send and smiled so hard she thought her face might fall off. Then Mae had another thought and she opened a second email. Checking the information Mitzey had put in her cell, she addressed the message to her new friend with the subject line: *To Be Opened on Christmas Eve Only!*

Dearest Mitzey,

Now you know what happens before anyone else too! Thank you so much for everything. Merry Christmas.

XOXO,
Mae

Mae attached a copy of the draft and sent it off to Mitzey. Completely reenergized, she turned to Scarpetta, who'd been laying by her food bowl as if hoping that the morning's excitement might lead to a second helping.

"You know what? I've just had another idea! Want to come to town with me?" Mae asked her faithful buddy. Scarpetta got up, having no idea what she was agreeing to, but Mae could tell she was definitely game as there could be snacks anywhere! Mae scribbled a brief note to her parents and the pair headed towards the hall where Mae grabbed her coat and bag. The two adventurers were ready to roll, again!

Mae parked in front of *Pass The Syrup,* a shop in town that sold fresh maple products and also specialized in things like beautiful pinecone arrangements.

"You want to stay or come in?" Mae asked Scarpetta, who didn't pick up her head, but only raised an eyeball. "OK, gotchu!" Mae laughed. She left the keys in the ignition to keep the heat on and the Christmas music going—it was New Hampshire after all. She cracked a window and then hopped out.

"Jinhae!" Mae greeted the man who was standing behind the counter dressed like a snazzy lumberjack. His mother had named him after a town in South Korea that apparently was famous for their Cherry Blossom festival. When Jinhae had told Mae that, she found it so fitting that he grew up to be so gifted with all things growing.

"Mae!" Her friend walked around the counter to come and give her a hug. "I heard you were back in town. Is it for a while?"

"For a big while, yeah! I brought everything back from LA with me. I'm helping my parents at the ski center!" Mae explained the move in a manner that no longer felt full of tension. "I'm going to fix up a writing room in the back and everything!"

"How exciting!" Jinhae exclaimed. "You get to do everything you love, and all in one place!"

"Yes!" Mae beamed, and she finally really felt it deep in her bones. "I get to do everything I love. Thank you!"

"Well, I am so glad to see you. Rob and I would love to have you over for dinner sometime, once you get settled in." He went back behind the counter. "Are you looking for anything in particular?"

"Actually! I was bragging about your maple syrup and I wanted to send some to a new friend," Mae said as she walked over to stand in front of the syrups that she knew Jinhae had tapped himself from their very own trees. She picked out one of the mini jugs. "I have to Next Day Air it so it will get there on time, but I'll of course come back for more larger sizes in the future! You know I think you guys have the best syrup ever. Like, ever!" Mae's eyes rested on the sweets section and her mind drifted to Jack. "You know what, I'll take a box of the Needhams as well. I have a, a new friend, who's never tried one. And you know what else, let's throw some of the maple candies in there too."

"Great!" Jinhae said as he wrapped up Mae's items. "Wonderful to see you, Mae. And, so happy!"

"Thank you," Mae said as she paid for her gifts. She smiled broadly, a new idea already formulating in her head. "Wonderful to see you too. Please give Rob my love!" Mae waved and turned to head out. As she neared the door Jinhae came from behind the register and jogged towards Mae, pausing briefly to grab something from a shelf.

"Mae!" He stopped her right as she was about to leave. "I would love for you to have these. A little something to celebrate the season." He handed Mae a pair of beautifully woven bright red mittens. "Merry Christmas!"

"Oh, Jinhae! This is so incredibly kind!" She looked down at the gorgeous mittens which felt so wonderfully soft in her hands and broke out into an even wider smile as she recalled her conversation with Julie. Well, she thought, they weren't a red jacket, but they would most certainly do. "Thank you!" she exclaimed and hugged her friend again. "Merry Christmas!"

After her triumphant visit to *Pass The Syrup,* Mae swung by the Post Office to mail the maple syrup to Rex. Scarpetta, again, had opted to stay in the vehicle and listen to music. Mae was at the packing table, going through her bag looking for the receipt from Rex's with his address on it, when Renee scooted in behind her.

"I saw Scarpetta in the Jeep. She told me you were here," Renee said as she gave Mae's bum a swat.

"She's always giving up all my secrets," Mae smiled. "I tried to bring her with me but it seems she'd rather listen to Bing Crosby."

"She really is a Robards!" They both looked out the window at the Jeep running outside. They could see Scarpetta laying across the back seat on a blanket with the heat on and the window cracked, like the most comfortable queen in the entire world.

"Thank you again, Renee, for coming by yesterday afternoon." Mae turned her attention back on her friend. "It was really, really wonderful. And... I finished!"

"You're finished! Oh wow! YES! I didn't doubt it for one second!" Renee exclaimed.

"I know you didn't, and I deeply appreciate that. Because I most certainly did. I don't think I could have gotten through these past couple of days without you all."

"Sure, you could have!" Renee interjected.

"No," Mae said firmly. "Well, not like this at least." The two women stood for a moment in acknowledgment of the deep friendship between them. Finally, Mae broke the silence. "OK, how was that for me sharing vulnerable mooshie feelings?! I feel kinda dirty." Mae laughed.

"YOU!" Renee swatted her bum again. "And speaking of, when does a certain someone come back to town?"

"I don't know exactly. I told him he could leave all his stuff in the cabin for as long as he wanted. He and my dad talked before he went up to check out the notch. Apparently, he was going for a couple of days and then would be back before Christmas. So..." Mae shrugged.

"I can only hope that I get to see him when he comes by. If he's not hiding from me because I acted like a total monster."

"A mostly delightful monster," Renee said as she laughed. "Well, Christmas IS a time for miracles!" she added gleefully. It had been a well-used phrase as of late.

"OK, we're getting pretty cheesy now!" Mae rolled her eyes like she loved to do. "Honestly, Renee, I used to be so cool," said Mae, pretending to act all serious.

"No. No, you didn't," Renee replied, always coming in with the truth.

"SO true!" Mae admitted rather merrily. "I was never cool."

"Which is actually what makes you so super cool," Renee said as the two friends broke out into what sounded like a fit of teenage laughter.

"Well, OK!" Mae said grabbing her package to ship and her red mittens. "I guess I might as well just commit to it then."

The Holiday Breakdown

Chapter 20 - A Disheveled Whimsey PST

Back in Los Angeles, Neal Michaels awoke to the sound of his girls, Amber and Alyssa, screaming with absolute delight. It was Christmas Eve Eve after all, and the entire house was full of excitement. He let them drag him out of bed and to the kitchen where they wanted to read him the notes that they were leaving for Santa. The girls, of course, had already mailed longer letters to the Big Man in Red earlier in the month, but they also liked to leave a follow-up message with the cookies just to make sure Santa knew how good they really had been.

"Give me one quick second girls," Neal said as he lifted Alyssa onto his leg. "I just have to check my messages very briefly and then I want to hear both your letters!" Neal turned on his phone in case Mae had already sent over the draft. He wasn't going to hold his breath—she did have until the end of the day. Much to his delight, he saw a message with an attachment waiting from Mae. As he went to open it a voicemail beeped through. He held the phone to his ear and broke into a huge smile as he heard Mae's message. He texted her back immediately:

Just got your VM and the draft. Will Fwd to Birk now. Can't wait to read. Congrats Mae!

After he sent the text to Mae and forwarded the draft to the editor, he turned back to his daughters grinning broadly.

"So, what do we have waiting for Santa?" His girls jumped up and down with their letters, excited to share them with their dad. It was going to be a wonderful Christmas!

Elizabeth Birk had woken up early and was enjoying the smell of the fresh wreath that had been recently hung in her home office. Steven had insisted that they not only get a tree for the main room, but also a few handsome wreaths to put in different areas of the house and, of course, one for the door out front. Elizabeth had acquiesced to all of Steven's strong suggestions as she'd been so nervous about Clare's surprise visit home. On the morning of the twenty-third Elizabeth hadn't wanted to wake her daughter, who had arrived late the night before, so she was staying in her office until Clare came down. Later that morning they were supposed to decorate the tree together, which currently only had lights on it as Elizabeth had saved the ornaments to do as a mother daughter date. She was seated at her desk when the email from Neal arrived. Elizabeth opened the message to check and see if the draft was attached. It was. She got up and walked over to the bookshelf where she kept all the novels that she'd read from the different publishers where she had worked. She dragged her fingers along the titles until she came upon one of Mae's and pulled it out. At that moment she heard a noise at the door and turned.

"Mom," Clare said rubbing her eyes. "I was just going to make more coffee. Do you want some?"

"Sure," Elizabeth smiled. "I'd love a refill."

"Oh, is that a Sarno novel?" Her daughter asked, stepping into the room and peering at the book in Elizabeth's hands.

"Yes. She is one of my writers at the publishing house I'm at now. Are you familiar?" Elizabeth asked curiously.

"Yes, in fact, she's probably my absolute favorite! That's so cool, mom!" Clare said enthusiastically, almost causing Elizabeth to turn pink. She couldn't remember the last time her daughter had called her cool. They had been on very rocky grounds ever since Clare was in high school and the rift had only gotten larger after she'd gone off to college. Elizabeth was a single mom and Clare was her world. However, it was possible, that at times Elizabeth had expressed that love not directly but instead by being, perhaps, a tad overly critical. She hadn't wanted Clare to have to deal with any of the challenges that she had dealt with. She had thought it would be easier for Clare if she didn't stand out so much. It was a lot to take on, going against the main current, Elizabeth knew that from experience. But maybe, she thought, that had ended up making Clare feel like who she was wasn't okay, which hadn't been her intention at all. She had just wanted to protect her. More than anything, Elizabeth wanted another chance to let Clare be exactly who she was and to enjoy each other.

"What do you like most about the books?" Elizabeth was excited to hear her daughter's opinion.

"Ummmmm...well," Clare started enthusiastically. "The main character is so, uh, delightfully disheveled, I guess is how I could describe it. There's a levity to her mischievousness that I love. Really different and special for a crime novel. And she still always figures it out! I guess I relate to the sort of frantic self-assessments and that someone who is so capable in so many ways, is really a mess in others. Maybe it makes me feel like being out of the ordinary is, uh, ok. Fun even. Like I can laugh at it. I don't know. I'd have to think about it to be more specific."

"No, that is absolutely perfect. Thank you, Clare!" Elizabeth looked back down at the book and then back at her daughter. "Start the coffee. I'll meet you in the living room and we'll decorate the tree if you'd like."

"Great!" Her daughter smiled, apparently as happy as Elizabeth was to start fresh. "I'll put on my favorite Muppets Christmas Album. Do you still have it?"

"The one with John Denver? Of course! It's on the shelf with all the vinyl. It's in alphabetical order, by genre." They both smiled, of course it was. Clare headed out to have her way with the record player and the coffee maker while Elizabeth sat back down at her desk. She shook her head; she had been so blind. Elizabeth opened the email from Neal and hit reply.

The Holiday Breakdown

Chapter 21 - Christmas Eve

*M*ae was seated at the table with her parents for dinner. She was feeling pretty good after the day's events and excited that tomorrow was Christmas Eve; it was one of her two most favorite days in the entire year (the other, of course, being Christmas).

"You remember The DeCiccos?" Her mom asked but didn't wait for an answer. "Well, they were originally The Cunninghams but then Robyn remarried. Anyway! I work with Robyn over at the Church Food Pantry and her eldest daughter, Dawn, is home from college and looking for work. Robyn thinks that Dawn would love to do the part-time trail maintenance until we find someone more permanent or until she goes back for the second semester."

"Great!" said Mae, very delighted hear it. She didn't know Dawn well, but had gone to high school with her older sister Meghan, who had moved to Massachusetts after school and opened her own construction company called *Cunningham Construction*. Mae was thoroughly impressed and loved getting the company emails, which she mostly enjoyed because of the pictures of Meghan standing on different kinds of equipment. Mae had grown up with some pretty cool women, she thought!

"Jack said he would let us know his timeframe as soon as he had all the details for the job," her father added, subtly reminding Mae (as if she had forgotten) that Jack was due to come back soon.

"So!" Mae started. "I had a possibly fun idea run through my mind today when I was at *Pass The Syrup*. I was thinking that some of the people driving through the area don't necessarily turn off to go into the town, but they do drive by us. So, maybe we could feature some of the goodies from the local shops. Like a little group advertising. Plus, it might get some people to pull in, even if they weren't planning to, if they saw signs for hot coffee and treats. I know that always works on me at least." Mae laughed at herself. "Then I thought, since we do have that big open space in the ski center, maybe we could even sell a few handcrafted items for people who don't have their own store fronts. A win-win for everyone. I mean, it wouldn't be a big push of the needle, but it would be a start."

"I think that's a great idea honey!" Gloria said enthused.

"Thanks mom!" Mae smiled broadly.

"Me too, Mae," her dad agreed.

"Great! I'll start floating it by some people in town after Christmas to see what everyone thinks," Mae said, excited to have her brain space back for incoming ideas. She had been stuck in writer's block doom and gloom town for so long and it was so great to feel like all her synapsis were firing again.

"OK. So!" Kurt Robards drummed on the table. "What are our plans for tomorrow? I do believe it's going to be Christmas Eve?!"

"Well, I do believe it is! I was going to get up early and make sure all the trails were in shape," Mae responded.

"Good idea. I heard there's a big snow coming!" her father said hopefully.

"Really?" Mae loved very few things more than a fresh snow.

"That's what the Farmer's Almanac gossip is!" Kurt Robards always tended to believe the almanac gossip, such as it was. "I was going to start the Christmas rolls and then I'll stay out front in case anyone comes by for passes or needs help with skis. Positive thinking and all."

"Maybe we should put a sign up that says we're not open on Christmas Day. We could even close a little early tomorrow? We don't want to have to rush getting dinner together and going to the 7pm service," her mother suggested.

"Sounds good to me!" Mae said. And it really did sound absolutely perfect. She just hoped with all her heart the Jack would make it to Christmas Eve dinner too.

The next morning Mae was out on the trails bright and early. Her dad (and the almanac) had been absolutely right. The air was thick and had a gleam to it that only occurred with an impending snow. She had just stopped skiing in order to fix her tool belt when a figure emerged from around the bend in the glowing light.

"Thank you, Santa," Mae whispered as she inhaled a grateful breath. She pushed off and skied towards the approaching man. "Jack!" she yelled and noticed again what a handsome silhouette he cast. The edge of her ski suddenly caught, but she righted herself before falling all the way over. Mae kept it moving though, wishing she could just keep it together for one time in her life.

"Mae!" Jack responded. "Your parents said you were out here! Seems like a lot has happened since I was gone."

"Yeah I..." Mae pulled to a stop beside him. "Well, first let me say that ummm... Jack I... I'm really sorry that I didn't let you talk, and I just steamrolled you out of the house. It was wrong of me. I thought you knew about the job earlier and had been keeping it from me because you were afraid to tell me, or maybe you weren't going to tell us at all, which didn't seem like you. I, of course, wanted you to take it. And, I didn't know that you'd already talked to my dad, and, anyway! I was way off and I overreacted. It was rude, and I'm sorry." Mae held in her breath waiting for Jack's response.

"Well, I accept your apology, Mae Robards. Thank you," Jack said sincerely. "Also, Mitzey said that you might have misheard a part of a phone conversation." He seemed to have a devious smile growing.

"What?!" Mae suddenly became even more flustered. "I wasn't eavesdropping. I was just coming to invite you to dinner and then you were on the phone. I immediately turned around to leave and then I accidentally heard a snippet. I'm sorry. I was embarrassed at the idea that you might only be staying out of obligation. And I, I don't know…"

"Next time you can just ask me," Jack stepped in a little closer.

"Seems so simple, doesn't it." Mae said as she heard her *YouAreSoFit* watch starting to beep again. Mortifying.

"Maybe I should get you a new watch for Christmas?" Jack said earnestly. "The batteries on yours always seem to be running out." He paused. "Looking back, I probably should have told you right after Derek called about the job offer, before talking about it with your parents, but you seemed like you were on such a roll with your writing. I didn't want to disrupt your flow."

"That's ok," said Mae. "I appreciate that."

"Also, I didn't have all the details yet for the job and I was kind of hoping I could stay a little longer… I like it here," Jack said looking directly into Mae's eyes. The temperature rose so swiftly inside Mae's snowsuit she thought she might need a fan. They were so close it was almost as if they were about to kiss.

"How did the interview go?" Mae asked totally ruining the intimate moment. Dang it, Mae, she thought.

"Did you like the base camp there? It's so nice over in the notch, right?" Mae heard her own voice babbling on about the notch and base camps and thought she sounded like she was someone's relative or school teacher addressing a student. Ehhhhh, she was the absolute worst!

"Yeah, it's very nice," Jack answered seeming not to notice Mae's inner battle. "I wanted to talk to you about it."

"OK!" Mae took in a deep breath, super casually (she hoped).

"They are offering me the job and I did accept it," Jack started.

"That's so great!" Mae said, really meaning it. She would be sad to see him leave right away but was so happy that this was working out for him.

"Thank you," Jack said, seeming very content with the situation. "It's not the same kind of job I am used to. It's people packing in and out. I would take supplies to the huts and deal with any emergencies that come up. I'd also cut trails starting in the spring. It's full-time but it's not regular hours."

"Oh, that seems so perfect for you!" Mae cheered.

"It really is," Jack agreed. He took a beat before starting again, "I would need a place to stay in between and on off times. I was thinking...well, I was wondering...how would you feel if I kept my stuff in the back? And in exchange for rooming, I could help you with the trails on days I'm here. Maybe Sammy could stay with you guys sometime... Is that too much to ask? I don't know." Jack actually looked slightly shy in that moment and Mae realized that he had never asked her for something or told her anything that he hoped for himself, outside of the job. Probably it took a lot of courage for him and she appreciated it immensely.

"That sounds wonderful actually," she said warmly.

"Oh, great. Great!" Jack seemed to relax. "The job doesn't start until after Christmas so maybe I can help you find someone to cover for when I'm not here."

"Thank you for the offer, but we can manage." Mae responded. "I think we might have someone who is home from college to help for a while."

"Oh," Jack said, suddenly seeming slightly let down. "OK. Well, Lori, Derek's wife, said I could spend Christmas out there with them if you guys had made other plans or whatever..." He trailed off.

"What? Oh, no. I mean, only if you want to. I meant you didn't have to help us look for anyone, but we would love for you to still spend Christmas with us." Mae corrected.

"That would be great!" Jack perked back up.

"We have a lot to celebrate," Mae said. "Your new job. And...I finished my book!"

"Mae that's wonderful, congratulations!" Jack seemed so genuinely happy for her that it warmed her all over again. "Tell me all about it!"

"Thank you! I'm really happy. It all came back, my rhythm I mean. Somehow, I had gotten so afraid that I was done forever. Like I'd forgotten how to write or something..." Such a huge weight was off Mae's chest. She felt like herself again, finally. She had so much she wanted to share with Jack that she was excited about. "AND, I thought of a few ideas for The Center. Like we could sell some items from people in town in the front lobby. We'll get a little bit of it, and it would help promote them, since people drive by here first mostly. Plus, it will be great for people who don't have a storefront but have things they want to put out. We have that big space. And Renee said she'd like to set up a station, we'll put *Hot Coffee* on the sign, maybe get some extra people pulling in to take a look."

"Great!"

"And then!" Mae continued. "This is a wild one…" She felt a little more hesitant about telling him about the audiobook idea because she felt so protective of it, but she wanted to share with Jack. "I was thinking about setting up a sound studio in the back so we can record my series as audiobooks."

"Mae!" Jack exclaimed. "That's a great idea!"

"Yay! Thank you. Sarah thought of it." Mae glowed. "That's one of my friends from LA."

"I really love it, Mae." Jack said earnestly. "I actually had a thought too. I was going to tell you right before…well…"

"Right before I flipped out on you?" Mae finished the sentence with her own version of events.

"Well, those weren't the words I was going to use," Jack smiled. "But, when I was going through the back trails, near that big opening by the brook, I was thinking you could build a little covering or gazebo there and advertise it as a place for gatherings and celebrations. That would involve what exactly, permits? I don't know, but…it's really beautiful out there and it's such a nice open space in the middle of the trees. Also, it would open you up for other seasons if you wanted."

"I absolutely love it! Awesome idea, Jack!" Mae thought it was a wonderful idea and felt confident that no matter what happened they were going to keep the ski center going strong. As she stood there, basking in a moment of positivity, it started to snow. "Maybe it is *White Christmas*," Mae murmured as she looked up into the falling flakes.

"What?" Jack asked as he gazed up into the snow himself.

"Oh, just something Mitzey said," Mae replied vaguely as she noticed the new snow was sticking to Jack's beautiful eyelashes. Suddenly her phone started ringing and she pulled it out of her tool belt to look. "I'm sorry Jack, it's Neal. I have to take it, we've been playing phone tag."

"Take it! Go!" Jack said to Mae and she took off skiing towards better cell service.

"Neal! Hey!" Mae answered the phone. "Wait, I can't hear you… I'm out in the woods. Hold on let me move closer to the house." She turned to Jack and pointed forward to illustrate where she was going. He waved back with a goooooooo motion. She shushed ahead, poles hanging off her wrists, phone to her ear. "What? Say it again Neal."

"…excited to read your new book and respects your Laela as is!" Neal's voice finally came through the phone clearly.

"Oh, my goodness!" Mae raised her phone-less hand and ski pole up in celebration. "Yay, us!"

"I thought it was some very nice news myself." Neal sounded delighted. "Congratulations Mae, you did it!"

"Thank you," Mae said, beaming. "Congratulations to you too, Neal. Merry Christmas."

"Merry Christmas, Mae!"

Mae hung up the phone, she was so excited that when she turned, wanting to yell the good news to Jack, she flipped around so quickly that her skis came out from underneath her and she butt planted right into the snow. Mae laid back on the ground laughing so hard at herself. Why even fight it, she thought? She was a tumultuous Christmas mess and she should just enjoy the ride.

Chapter 22 - The Protagonist in a Christmas Romance

*T*he Reverend Woods opened the Church doors to let the parishioners out into the falling snow. The congregation slowly exited while singing *Silent Night,* their candle wicks burning brightly on this gorgeous Christmas Eve. As the song ended, everyone stood for a moment and then blew out their candles before turning to wish each other a Merry Christmas.

Gloria, Kurt, Jack, and Mae all headed back towards their vehicles. Mae's parents had taken a separate car as her mom had wanted to leave for early so she could drop off a few gifts to friends and see if they needed help setting anything up for the service.

"Meet you back at home," her dad said as he and Mae's mom climbed into their car.

"OK," Mae responded waving. Her Jeep was a little farther down the road so she and Jack continued walking in the falling snow. Mae's hands were warm inside the bright red Christmas mittens. She looked down at them and smiled. "I got a message back from Mitzey," she told Jack. "I had mailed Rex a little New Hampshire maple syrup in hopes that it was the motivation he needed to invite himself over for some holiday breakfast. Anyway! Mitzey updated me saying that Rex had asked her if it was OK if he joined her for Christmas and she seemed VERY excited about it so…"

"Your plan is unfolding perfectly," Jack laughed heartily.

"It would seem so! And, we have a fun morning to look forward to as well. I warned you in advance that you were entering Robards' Christmas Land, so be prepared. There will be the special holiday rolls, stockings, and…"

"Stockings?!" Jack stopped walking. "For me?"

"Of course! I believe there is one for both you and Sammy," Mae said as she turned to him. "Don't you think Santa makes it to New Hampshire?"

"Mae I…" Jack paused and took a step closer. Mae shivered, not from the cold but because they were mere inches apart, centimeters if they were in England or anywhere else in the world for that matter, Mae thought. Shrouded in a circle of light from the falling snow, Mae noticed how the gorgeous flakes were collecting on his hat, further illuminating those beautiful brown eyes. She saw that his lips were parting as he started to speak again. "You have all been so kind. This is…" But he was interrupted as Mae took a step closer and put a tentative but determined red mitten on the back of his head. She tilted her face up to him and gently pressed her mouth to his. His lips were so warm that they set Mae's skin ablaze, and she briefly wondered if all the snow that had landed on her was instantaneously melting off or if it was just her imagination. Mae felt his hand come up to hold the side of her neck as Jack passionately kissed her back. JINGLE BELLS! Holiday lights exploded in Mae's brain. It was a Christmas romance after all!

I would like to sincerely thank Amber Gavin for all your incredible efforts and time (you are absolute magic and I'm the luckiest for having you as a friend), Mark Masters for your amazing help (thank youuuuu SO MUCH), Brett Carducci for your aid and encouragement of my holiday obsession, Nick Leighton for your kind support, Meghan Hanley & Koral Fraser for your unmatched enthusiasm (it really means so much to me), Robyn Schall, Corinne Fisher, Calise Hawkins, Candi Clare, Regina DeCicco, Erin Jackson, Katie Novotny, Julie Rosing, Helen Hong, Brendan Fitzgibbons, Kristen Hartley, Giulia Rozzi, Charles McBee, Caitlin Peluffo & the *Were You Raised By Wolves* fam for your amazing shoutouts (xoxoxoxoxoxo), Kendra Cunningham for reading the original and rallying me to write a novel (you are too good and it is an honor to comedy and life with you), my parents for instilling in me a tremendous amount of Christmas Spirit (I love you), and Dustin Chafin for being my Samwise Gamgee and the best tow man that a girl could ask for.

Leah Bonnema is a comedian who lives in Los Angeles with her fiancé and their dog, Lacey Jane. She loves Christmas, the snowy woods and The Lord of the Rings. For more information, please go to LeahBonnema.com and follow her on Instagram @LeahBonnema.

Made in the USA
Las Vegas, NV
25 October 2022